DATE DUE

DEMCO 38-296

Mediation
in Contemporary
Native American
Fiction

—◆—

American Indian Literature
and
Critical Studies Series

Gerald Vizenor and Louis Owens, General Editors

Mediation in Contemporary Native American Fiction

◆

By James Ruppert

University of Oklahoma Press
Norman and London

A version of chapter 1 appeared in *Genre* 25 (1992):321–37. A version of chapters 1 and 2 appeared in *Texas Studies in Literature and Language* 28 (1986): 209–225. ©1986 by University of Texas Press. A version of chapter 5 appeared in *The Explicator*, vol. 51, no. 2, winter 1993, pp. 129–134. Reprinted with permission of the Helen Dwight Reid Educational Foundation. Published by Heldref Publications, 1319 18th Street, N.W., Washington D.C. 20036-1802. Copyright 1993. A version of Chapter 8 appeared in *North Dakota Quarterly* 59 (1991): 229–42.

This book is published with the generous assistance of the Kerr Foundation, Inc.

Ruppert, James, 1947–
    Mediation in contemporary Native American fiction / by James Ruppert.
    p.   cm. — (American Indian literature and critical studies series ; v. 15)
    Includes index.
    ISBN 0-8061-2749-X
    1. American fiction — Indian authors — History and criticism.   2. American fiction — 20th century — History and criticism.   3. Indians of North America in literature.   4. Mediation in literature.   I. Title.   II. Series.
    PS374.I49R87   1995
    813'.5409897 — dc20   94-47465
                                                                                                 CIP

Mediation in Contemporary Native American Fiction is Volume 15 in the American Indian Literature and Critical Studies Series.

The paper in this book meets the guidelines for permanence and durability of the Committee on Production Guidelines for Book Longevity of the Council on Library Resources, Inc. ∞

1   2   3   4   5   6   7   8   9   10

Contents

Introduction

◆

an appreciation for the boundless capacity of language which,
through storytelling, brings us together, despite great distances
between cultures, despite great distances in time.
—Leslie Silko

I have always found Silko's belief in language and storytelling
to be infectious. My personal experience over the years has
only confirmed her insight. My hope is that some of the
appreciation for language and storytelling that Native writers
have taught me can be carried over into this book, and move
readers a little closer to such acts that bring us together. No
greater appreciation could inform a book on Native American
literature. My own journey has been to cross those distances
of time and culture to which Silko refers. Over twenty years
of experience with students, writers, and educators, but
especially Native students and writers, form the basis of this
book. From the 1970s on I have been enriched by my friend-
ships with Native writers, and I have learned as much from
my Native students as I have taught. While the criticism I read
in the 1970s continually mentioned the agony of Native peoples existing between two worlds, the writers I knew did not

seem to me to be people lost between two worlds, nor any more agonized than most people, but rather they were able to call up the richness of a mixed heritage and see things in ways new to both traditions. My critical work since then has been an attempt to understand something of that rich potential, to develop the appreciation of which Silko wrote. Teaching Native American literature to classes of exclusively Native students or to classes with Native and non-Native students has given me some insight into how various readers respond to a few of the major texts in this field and into the roles assigned to readers by the texts. I have tried to carry to this book a little of what those students taught me.

These experiences have led me to theorize about a generative position of contemporary Native writers that I call *mediation* and to consider the multiple narratives of identity that their texts create. It has become clear to me that wider, more inclusive definitions of identity are necessary before an adequate understanding of these texts can take place. I agree with Michael Fischer when he writes, "Ethnicity is not something that is simply passed on from generation to generation, taught and learned; it is something dynamic, often unsuccessfully repressed or avoided" (195). As the dynamic quality of this identity in the making is encoded in the texts of contemporary Native American literature, readers from various backgrounds are brought into the process. I have seen this response triggered in many students. They meet a literature in a dynamic struggle to define its identity and cannot help but let it touch their own efforts to see themselves. As Fischer further reflects, this literature can initiate for readers, "a dialectical or two-sided journey examining the realities of both sides of cultural differences so that they may mutually question each other, and thereby generate a realistic image of human possibilities and a self-confidence for the explorer grounded in comparative understanding rather than ethnocentrism" (217). Because of this potential for reinvigoration and reinspiration, I find Native American literature the most stimulating and exciting component of contemporary literature.

From my point of view, this reinvigoration can only be detected in a reader implied by the text, certainly not in the text itself. Whether as a result of a different world view, the influence of the oral tradition, or the politics of marginalization, the contemporary Native American novel is oriented toward a restructuring of the readers' preconceptions and expectations. Yet it would seem that the message orientation of the protest novel is too constricting for Native writers, who often see themselves as changing the way people think and understand. Elaine Jahner expresses this idea when she writes that the emerging American Indian novel was, "one that has interesting differences from other types of American novels because its emphasis is less on what is known than on how one comes to know certain things and because it demands an attentiveness from the reader that has less to do with grasping what the action is than it does with feeling how actions have meanings that live and grow according to the many different ways human beings have of knowing about them" ("Act" 45). In my discussion of some of the best known and most widely read contemporary Native American novels my goal has been to explore how the texts maneuver the readers into these different ways of knowing. The six novels chosen for discussion are the most commonly taught and discussed, and thus if my analysis has anything to add to the variety of theoretical approaches to Native American Literature, these novels form the testing grounds.

However, to explore completely the role of the implied reader, I have found it necessary to acknowledge the role of both Native and non-Native reader. The role of such readers can be deduced by reference to linguistic, epistemological, and sociopolitical contexts and fields of discourse. Such an approach also requires an acknowledgment of a high level of intertextuality between outside fields of discourse as well as inside fields of discourse, for readers are expected to move between Native and non-Native discourse to varying degrees. This kind of movement can be a formidable task for the reader, the writer, and the scholar.

Perhaps that is the reason scholars have often tended to emphasize either the rootedness of the Native American novel in culture or its connections to modern Western literary traditions. I desire here to develop a methodology that makes use of illuminating contextual material when called for as well as contemporary literary theory. I hope to avoid the one-dimensional approach against which Reed Way Dasenbrock warns, "The temptation in studying such bicultural writers is to deny their biculturality, to privilege one of their formative cultures in the name of authenticity or the other in the name of universality. And the temptation is stronger when the cultures are so obviously not fused but still separate and in a state of tension and interaction" (317). He might also add, when the cultures are separated by mutually acknowledged world views and epistemologies. Thus the scholar must be as concerned with balance as the novelist is. Indeed much of what Arnold Krupat has written concerning *ethnocriticism* emphasizes the necessary transcultural nature of a new criticism of Native American materials, believing that this balanced scholarship "will only be achieved by means of complex interactions between a variety of Western discursive and analytical modes and a variety of non-Western modes of knowing and understanding" (*Ethnocriticism* 44).

Contemporary Native American novelists do more than create representations of bicultural experience. Their works may grow out of Western literary forms, but they are forms being used for Native purposes that may vary from negating stereotypes to emphasizing cultural survival. In essence, they set up a dialogic relationship between Native and non-Native discourse fields to disrupt the easy engagement of the dominant literary discourse. These works create what Mary Louise Pratt has called the "contact zone." For her, such works might be considered autoethnographic, since they engage with representations others have made of them. . . . [they] are representations that the so-defined others construct *in response to* or in dialogue with those texts. Autoethnographic texts are not, then, what are usually thought of as autochthonous forms of expression or self-representation. . . . Rather they involve a selective collaboration with and appropriation of idioms of the metropolis or the conqueror. These are merged or infiltrated to varying degrees with indigenous idioms to create self-representations intended to intervene in metropolitan modes of understanding. Autoethnographic works are often addressed to both metropolitan audiences and the speaker's own community. Thus their reception is highly indeterminate. (35)

My method is to observe how such works address implied audiences and to explore how the self-representations intervene in metropolitan modes of understanding. However, implicit in my approach is the belief that such works do not merely mouth expected statements familiar to the speaker's community, but that they require new insights, sometimes conditioned by the idioms of the metropolis, to complete the work of mediation.

In this light, the mediation of the texts could be seen as self-reflexive and thus in keeping with postmodern literature's expectation of self-conscious narration. Indeed there are a number of ways in which contemporary Native American literature is in the forefront of postmodern literature. Its sources in oral tradition push for a literature in which story becomes reality, in which objective claims of truth give way to narrative as essential to understanding and meaning. The emergence of the voice of the *Other* in these novels serves a postmodern political purpose by moving marginalized experience to the center, by legitimatizing that which Western culture has sought to delegitimatize. Postmodern attempts to deconstruct the illusion of authority and inevitableness inherent in Western discourses about truth and meaning may find allies in the world of Native American literature. Gerald Vizenor also thinks that many elements of the novels reveal a postmodern condition: "Linear time is abolished, the myth of time being present. Dreams are a source of reality as much as any other experience, and that is postmodern. Stories are never told in the same way. Each telling is a different story, a different condition, a different instance of encounter, and that is postmodern" ("GERALD" 113). Especially for Vizenor's work, the transformational matrix of his characters and their stories could be seen as exemplifying postmodern concerns. Yet in many other ways contemporary Native American literature is unconcerned with postmodern questions. I agree with Louis Owens when he writes of Native American writers, "They work for the most part consciously outside the concerns of postmodern theoretists, at times working at odds with the aims of deconstructionist theory" (*Other* 19). If the postmodern is characterized, as Jean-François Lyotard suggests, by incredulity toward the metanarrative and a belief in the liberating qualities of fragmentary and iconoclastic narratives, then Native American writers seem decidedly non-postmodern.[1] Much of the work of contemporary Native writers incorporates an overriding metanarrative and often mythic structure through which the narrative, the characters, and the readers find meaning. It seems that much of the work is characterized by a historical vision, a sense of social responsibility and a belief in the efficacy of the word — qualities not to be found in postmodern literature. From Silko to Vizenor, this is a literature with a purpose.

Perhaps a few general comments on criticism and the scholarship in this book would be appropriate here. I have not intended that my discussions be considered definitive or exhaustive. My wish is not to survey the works of the writers included nor to discuss every aspect of the novels considered. Rather, I have a line of thought I wanted to work out on a large scale. I think of the scholarship here as a contribution to a growing and exciting field of study. I have tried to demonstrate the ways in which my research is part of an ongoing discussion about these novels as well as the ways in which my perspective is a response to those of other scholars and writers.

When I think of critical activity in terms of truth, authenticity, and objectivity, I am often guided by the insights of Hannah Arendt in her essay, "The Concept of History." Among other topics, she brings Heisenberg's writings to bear on historical scholarship. While deconstructing the concept of objective truth, she demonstrates (and here I am simplifying grossly) that experimentation and research are activities that start with questions consistent in a system and conclude with answers consistent in that system. Other questions are possible when one applies another system with other possible answers. No one set of answers can claim absolute truth or definitiveness. This book is a set of answers to my questions. The questions have helped me think about these works of fiction and have proved useful in the classroom. I hope others will also find some value in this line of thought as they make up their own questions.

Mediation
in Contemporary
Native American
Fiction

1

Mediation

◆

Contemporary Native American artists are in a position full of potential. As participants in two cultural traditions, they pattern their art with discursive acts of mediation at many levels. By mediation, I mean an artistic and conceptual standpoint, constantly flexible, which uses the epistemological frameworks of Native American and Western cultural traditions to illuminate and enrich each other.[1] In working toward an understanding of Native American writers' texts, it is more useful to see them not as between two cultures (a romantic and victimist perspective) but as participants in two rich cultural traditions. While some may say these writers are apologists for one side or the other, or that their texts inhabit a no-man's-land, a mediational approach explores how their texts create a dynamic that brings differing cultural codes into confluence to reinforce and re-create the structures of human life: the self, community, spirit, and the world we perceive. Through their mediating position, the writers are "protecting and celebrating the cores of cultures left in the wake of catastrophe" (Erdrich, "Where" 23).

They may dismantle European American stereotypes, create cultural criticism of the dominant society, and make manifest the crimes of the past, but their mediational goals direct them more toward Native concerns such as nurturing survival, continuance, and continual reemergence of cultural identity. As Vizenor has written in his unique style, "Native American Indian literatures are tribal discourse, more discourse. The oral and written narratives are language games, comic discourse rather than mere responses to colonialist demands or social science theories" ("Postmodern" 4). For many scholars only the social tragedy in contemporary Native American Literature has been important. The works function, according to such scholars, to represent the colonization of Native peoples. However, the texts clearly reject victimizing literary interpretations from one-dimensional Western perspectives.

On the other hand, it is all too obvious that contemporary Native American fiction, poetry, and drama conform to many Western expectations and present characters who can be understood in terms of Western psychology and sociology. But James Clifford suggests that even our conceptions of cultural continuity may be inadequate to the understanding of contemporary Native American experience. Thus, in texts by contemporary Native writers, "Metaphors of continuity and 'survival' do not account for complex historical processes of appropriation, compromise, subversion, masking, invention, and revival" (338). But perhaps most difficult and yet potentially illuminating can be the realization of how Native goals and tribal discourse can coexist with more Western goals in the text and texture of these works. An exploration of how Hyemeyohsts Storm's *Seven Arrows* engages contemporary European/American social discourse of the 1960s might be as revealing as a discussion of Chippewa vision discourse in Gerald Vizenor's *Bearheart: The Heirship Chronicles*.

Much necessary and solid research has been done establishing the cultural references of contemporary Native American Literature. But historical and textual scholars have combined with more anthropologically minded scholars to downplay the contemporary literary discourse in the texts. Too often the attitude has been that to participate in the text, one must read an anthropologist first, turning the critical activity into what Andrew Wiget calls "a kind of shadow anthropology" ("Identity" 259). Some sociological reactionary criticism has even explored the texts solely in terms of how they respond to American attitudes toward assimilation. No scholar has explored in depth the question of multiple audiences, and the attempts to apply current literary theory or comparativist approaches have often been discounted by reviewers. A mediational methodology is designed to appreciate contemporary Native American literary works as bicultural texts patterning an active encounter with distinct audiences.

In discussing Native American literature, Paula Gunn Allen directs our attention to the mediational quality of contemporary texts and to some of their Native directions. She perceives contemporary Native American novels as becoming increasingly concerned with tribal and urban life. Though their narrative plotting is Western, they are essentially ritualistic in approach, structure, theme, symbol, and significance. They "rely on native rather than non-Indian forms, themes, and symbols and so are not colonial or exploitative. Rather they carry on the oral tradition at many levels, furthering and nourishing it and being furthered and nourished by it" (*Sacred* 79). Simon Ortiz sees no necessary conflict in the employment of Western literary forms. For him contemporary mediational texts may express both traditional goals and a new literary tradition. He writes "of the creative ability of Indian people to gather in many forms of the socio-political colonizing force which beset them and to make these forms meaningful in their own terms. . . . They [Western forms] are now Indian because of the creative development that the native people applied to them" ("Toward" 8).[2] Both of these writers speak eloquently of the potential of the author's mediative positioning, while choosing to emphasize the ultimate Native goals of their own writings and that done by their contemporaries.

Looking at the same body of work, Arnold Krupat sees the mediational mix as "influenced in a very substantial degree by the central forms of Western, or first world literature." He calls what I refer to as contemporary Native American Literature *indigenous literature*. For Krupat the work of Silko, Momaday, and others, "manages successfully to merge forms internal to his [the Native writer's] cultural formation with forms external to it, but pressing upon, even seeking to delegitimate it" (*Voice* 214). What each critic sees, though from a different perspective, is the same as what each reader perceives — the constantly changing texture of mediation, the possibilities of realigning and reinforcing the reader's epistemology. The successful contemporary Native writer can create a text that merges delegitimizing influences while continuing oral tradition and culture. The text is both substantially Native and substantially Western. In seeking its complex goals, it must adopt and transfer each culture's means of knowledge and value formation. This back and forth, the assertion and reassertion of value and form, creates multidimensional understanding for each reader. The best work of Momaday, Silko, Welch, Vizenor, Allen, and many others mediates as it illuminates, juxtaposing cultural traditions on both conscious and unconscious levels.

Yet these writers know that a writer cannot guarantee the reactions of real readers. Consequently the texts they generate assign roles for Native and non-Native readers to assume. The concept of the implied reader as outlined by Wolfgang Iser is useful here as a way of reminding us that writers expect readers to respond in certain ways, such as to laugh, be curious, or be afraid, even if they know they cannot completely manipulate them. Iser elaborates on this insight with his discussions of textual perspectives, finding the role of the implied reader inherent in the text.[3] Gerard Genette further specifies that the implied reader, often consisting "wholly of the signs that imply and sometimes designate him," can be deduced "by the competence—linguistic and narrative, among other kinds—that the text postulates in expecting to be read" (148–49).[4] Contemporary Native American writers construct implied readers through the textual perspective presupposed and through the narrative competence required, but also, because they are moving from one world view to another, implied readers require certain epistemological competence at various points in the text. The writers hope that the readers will assume these roles. To secure as much of a fusion between real and implied readers as possible, it is often the case that integrated meaning can only be achieved when the fusion is complete. In later chapters, I hope to demonstrate how these implied readers are forged, especially how they engage the discourse fields that contextualize the text.

As the writer strives to bring the oral into the written, the Native American vision into Western thinking, spirit into modern identity, community into society, and myth into modern imagination, he or she is not confined to one cultural framework. While Native American writers do create devastating critiques of European American society, they express wider and deeper concerns than those of social criticism. Nor are they limited to a self-congratulatory view that all the old traditions, the old ways of perceiving are immutable and omnipotent. Contemporary Native American writers insist on their freedom to use the forms and expectations of both Native and Western cultural codes to achieve the goals of each as well as to satisfy the epistemological expectations of both audiences. In *House Made of Dawn*, N. Scott Momaday, for instance, feels free to use both Native ceremonial ritual and modern literary stream of consciousness to set the implied reader's perceptual basis for mythic and sociological identity. As a participant in two literary and cultural traditions, Western and Native, the contemporary Native American writer is free to use the epistemological structures of one to penetrate the other, to stay within one cultural framework, or to change twice on the same page. While terms like *Western* and *Native* establish large generalizations that could be considered to undermine cultural diversity in each arena, such generalizations serve to point the student of contemporary Native American literature in useful directions. By *Western*, I refer to those cultural backgrounds in common with the various groups of Europe and America. By *Native*, I refer to the specific Native American cultural traditions with which the Native writer identifies and any areas of commonality between the many other cultural traditions.

In an essay on Acoma poet Simon Ortiz, Kenneth Lincoln sees this utilization of two cultures in terms of past and present: "Being Indian involves not just the traditions or catastrophes served up on a buffalo chip of history, but a conscious set of choices. The central issue is what to fuse of the new and the old, improvisations and continuances from the past" ("Common" 83). For Native American writers, mediation is expressed through their artistic choices and is vital to the continuance of identity.

By reminding us of the chronological dimension of the alternating use of world views and ways of knowing in mediational texts, Lincoln draws our attention to the way in which the mediative text is embedded in the context of all other discourses that have occurred in Western and Native traditions, discourses at once artistic, historical, and cultural. As discourse, the text is connected to other discourses through what James Clifford refers to as "the intersubjectivity of all speech" (41) and what Tzvetan Todorov, interpreting Mikhail Bakhtin, calls "intertextuality" (Bakhtin 60). Clifford, Todorov, and Bakhtin each in their own way call attention to how every discourse enters into relation with past discourses and expected future discourses, thereby vastly expanding a definition of the word *discourse* such as this one given by Julia Kristeva: "any enunciation that integrates in its structure the locutor and the listener, with the desire of the former to influence the latter" (1). Bakhtin asserts that "the dialogic orientation is obviously a characteristic phenomenon of all discourse. It is the natural aim of all living discourse. Discourse comes upon the discourse of the other on all the roads that lead to its object, and it cannot but enter into intense and lively interaction with it" (qtd. in Todorov, *Bakhtin* 62). Contemporary Native American writers may evoke a number of discourse fields from Western and Native traditions. Mediation, then, doubles the contexts and spheres of discourse since it moves from one cultural tradition to another as well as connecting the locutor to the listener.

One of the major paths toward the creation of a mediative text is through fusing and realigning the cultural patterns of discourse into the many elements of the text. The writer's sources run both chronologically through one sphere and cross-culturally between fields of discourse. In choosing "what to fuse of the old and the new," the writer decides how to engage previous discourse so that he or she will further its development and yet reveal how that sphere of discourse might find new ways of creating meaning, new ways of talking about what is meaningful inside its own field and other fields. In *Love Medicine*, Louise Erdrich uses oral tradition through personal narratives and symbolic, almost mythic, events current with the lives of her characters to engage the ongoing discourse of particular families while embedding in it larger and older fields of discourse. While implied non-Native readers recognize the form, they are led to question the assumptions about spiritual and communal meaning that underlie the discourse; on the other hand, implied Native readers must reevaluate the efficacy of such divergent discourse in creating continuing identity. The dynamic of mediation is similar to Michael Holquist's definition of Bakhtin's dialogism as a condition in which "everything means, is understood, as a part of a greater whole—there is a constant interaction between meanings, all of which have the potential of conditioning others" (Bakhtin 426).

The necessity for mediation to reach out of a cultural framework to achieve its goals forces an element of self-reflexiveness into the text. The writer is prompted to consider the logic of presentation of cultural values, the questions of world view, and the presence of differing audiences as the text creates an ideological position in larger cultural conversations. Donald Bialostosky sees this self-reflexiveness in dialogic conversation because:

> those who take turns speaking and listening, representing others and being represented by them, learn not just who these others are but who they themselves may be, not just what others may mean but what they themselves may mean among others. Whether the purview of such a conversation is a discipline, a culture, or a world of diverse cultures (and boundaries among these purviews are not fixed and given in any case), the dialogic participants will both make it what it is and be made by it, conferring identities on their fellows and their communities, even as they receive identities from them. (792)

In the case of contemporary Native American literature, the purview is both cultural and transcultural. Accordingly the cultural conversations engaged allow writers not only the chance to participate in a number of conversations but also to see what they mean among others both inside their cultural conversations and across unfixed boundaries. Native writers encourage implied readers to enter into conversations with which they are familiar and those with which they are not. However, no one ever has the last word. Each textual utterance awaits response and reinterpretation.

Consequently, the mediative enterprise strives to be as self-critical of its perception and form as it is critical of other perceptions and forms. The act of mediation throws into doubt all epistemological laws, even those governing its own formation, at least temporarily. Since mediation is as much about how we know and make meaning as it is about the social and cultural subjects delineated, it must tend toward metadiscursive reflexiveness as it weaves the locutor and the listener into that inclusive cultural web. In his discussion of discourse, Hayden White describes how discourse is always as much about interpretation as it is about the subject:

> A discourse moves "to and fro" between received encodations of experience and the clutter of phenomena which refuses incorporation into conventional notions of "reality," "truth," or "possibility." It also moves "back and forth" (like a shuttle) between alternative ways of encoding this reality, some of which may be provided by the traditions of discourse prevailing in a given domain of inquiry and others of which may be idiolects of the author, the authority of which he is seeking to establish. Discourse, in a word, is quintessentially a *mediative* enterprise. As such, it is both interpretive and preinterpretive; it is always as much *about* the nature of interpretation itself as it is *about* the subject matter which is the manifest occasion of its own elaboration. (4)

As the mediational text moves back and forth between "ways of encoding this reality," implied readers reevaluate interpretation, are informed, and can be changed as they try on alternate epistemologies, different cultural goals, and different notions of reality and truth. While readers attempt to encode those phenomena that resist incorporation into their predisposed beliefs, the Native American writer offers reconstructed ways of encoding experience based on traditional and contemporary insight into both cultures. The mediational text endeavors to move the readers implied by the text to question the way they form knowledge and meaning, but in the end it seeks to re-educate those readers so that they can understand two codes, two traditions of discourse. In short, texts aspire to change readers. The more complete the fusion between the implied reader and the real reader, the more complete the change. Yet neither the writer nor the readers can completely escape the metadiscursive reflexiveness of the text that at one moment and for one reader highlights an element of one cultural code while simultaneously backgrounding it for another reader with a different cultural tradition.

It might be fruitful here to point out that this metadiscursive reflexiveness has been a prominent feature of postmodern American literature, at least since the prominence of the writers of fabulation and metafiction in the 1970s. This fact, of course, has not escaped the notice of contemporary Native American writers. Equally well known to Native writers is the phenomenon that Dennis Tedlock has presented to non-Natives of storytelling in the oral tradition that establishes a dialectical relationship between "text and interpretation" (236). The interpretative and self-reflexive mode of oral discourse pervades the text, texture, and context of an oral event. This aspect of storytelling unites it with postmodern American literature. On this intermediate common ground, Native American oral tradition and contemporary American literature can meet. Thus, Allen's contention that contemporary Native writing can both nourish oral tradition and be nourished by it gains support.

As implied readers move from one world view to another, from one field of discourse to another, back and forth through the chronological depths of those fields and between text and interpretation, they are led to adopt a perspective on the meaning of the text, but this perspective is constantly changing, constantly being modified by a completely different set of epistemological codes. They cannot help but ask themselves if their understanding of previous moments in the reading of the text was correct. Iser describes the manner in which a reader moves through a text, a manner that becomes central to the success of a mediational text: "The reader's communication with the text is a dynamic process of self-correction, as he formulates signifieds which he must continually modify" (67). This formation and reformation of signifieds Iser calls misreading. As we read and then suspect we have misread, our perspective on all that has come before in the text changes. Through the process of reading the text, readers become something, someone they were not before. But more than that, if readers are open to the successful mediational text, they will tend to question their set of culturally determined assumptions about narrative, meaning, and life. Wallace Martin in his discussion of Iser's theories concludes:

> When a perspective on life proves inadequate, the reader tends to question the entire repertoire of conventional assumptions on which it is based. In Iser's view, narration progresses as a negation of partial and inadequate ways of understanding the world, leaving in its wake not a constructed meaning but a variety of hypothetical viewpoints depending on how the reader has filled in meanings, questioned social practices, and tried to find positive alternatives to the inadequate views represented in the text. If open to the experience the text provides, we are likely to find negations of some of our own views; as a result, the self that begins reading a book may not be quite the same self as the one that finishes it. (162)

Readers who finish a mediational text by a contemporary Native American writer will have been encouraged to examine not only their perspectives, but also their epistemology as they move back and forth in Native cultural conversations and between Native and non-Native cultural codes. The end result is that they are now open to a Native epistemological pattern that they previously did not know how to see and to the new hybrid forms of meaning and knowledge that contemporary Native American writers can create. One example is the ending of *Wind from an Enemy Sky*. D'Arcy McNickle presents readers with an unexpected tragedy that arises from the good motives of both whites and Indians. The tragedy continues a historical conflict and is prophesied by a spiritual leader's vision. However, this ending makes no sense in traditional narrative expectations and comes as a shock. Readers struggle to find the meaning in it; they question why they did not know it was coming, even though it had been foreshadowed. They start to rethink what they have seen as meaningful events and logical behavior. They contemplate how they can act to avoid such a tragedy. In the reader's conclusions rest the fruits of mediation.

Contemporary fiction seems ideally suited to achieving this epistemological restructuring.[5] Elaine Jahner argues that for the traditional storytellers, narratives were valued more as explorations of particular ways of knowing and learning than as static constructs of knowledge. Contemporary Native American storytellers often choose novels because "the novel is a narrative genre well-suited for examining how the traditional ways of knowing function in a multi-cultural world where the meanings of narrative are often twisted and tangled" ("Act" 45). The size and scope of the novel allows it the flexibility to juxtapose various narrative forms and then bring implied readers to a standoint where they can untangle their responses and misreadings, taking them back to their experiential roots. Since implies readers exist in a condition which is both self-reflexive and creative, real readers are more open to facing the Other and themselves in the Other; they read and form hypotheses about meaning only to have those revised and their methods questioned. Mikhail Bakhtin refers to this process as "ideological translation": "In a word, the novelistic plot serves to represent speaking persons and their ideological worlds. What is realized in the novel is the process of coming to know one's own language as it is perceived in someone else's system. There takes place within the novel an ideological translation of another's language, and an overcoming of its otherness—an otherness that is only contingent, external, illusory" (365). The process that Bakhtin describes for the novel equally describes mediational texts. Mediation produces a text in which various languages contend and are mutually translated. By language, Bakhtin means a sphere of discourse with a dynamic chronological dimension that defines an identity and ideological position. As the reader's language is translated, his or her self-conception and cultural code become translated; conceptions of

Native and Western discourse and identity are then seen through someone else's system. The implied Native reader sees through the non-Native; the implied non-Native reader sees through the Native. An implied reader of a mediational text must conclude by the end of a text that his or her understanding is complete and adequate even though it has been challenged and is now altered. In that sense, the Otherness has been illusory. The mediational world of the text may supply a place to assimilate the Other where the physical world may not. However it is not a world divorced from the political realities of contemporary Native American experience. As Bakhtin writes, "A dialogue of languages is a dialogue of social forces" (365). A mediational text attempts to maneuver readers into taking a series of regenerated sociopolitical positions. An ideological translation takes place, though not a physical transmutation, but, real readers may be ready to act because they perceive things differently.

What generates this mediation of the text is not only the Native writer's bicultural heritage but also the existence of multiple audiences. Native American writers write for two audiences—non-Native and Native American—or in many cases three audiences—a local one, a pan-tribal one, and a non-Native contemporary American one. The attempt to satisfy those audiences generates the peculiar construct of the Native writer's art. Contemporary Native writers want more than merely to stand between two cultures satisfying first one audience's expectations and then the other's. Such discourse would not develop much unity. And, such a creative stance would only tend to reinforce each cultural code rather than illuminate both. To illuminate and mediate, they utilize the different cultural codes simultaneously, for then surprise and meaning will be created by the implied reader, as he or she overcomes the momentary and illusory confusion of meeting the Other. Such a position is the most viable one for a Native American writer who wishes to decline the invitation to schizophrenia inherent in participating in two opposing cultural traditions.

Such a position also presents unparalleled potential for interpretation and synthesis. Allen theorizes that contemporary American Indians are always faced with a "dual perception of the world." Because Native writers feel compelled to explore how contemporary Native experience generates comprehensible patterns of life, they create a generative artistic discourse "that will not only reflect the dual perceptions of Indian/non-Indian but will reconcile them. The ideal metaphor will harmonize the contradictions and balance them so that internal equilibrium can be achieved, so that each perspective is meaningful, and in their joining psychic unity rather than fragmentation occurs" (*Sacred* 161). For Allen, the successful mediation harmonizes the contradictions, creating unity and legitimatizing both spheres of discourse.

Too much criticism of contemporary Native American writing has applied the epistemological expectations of only one cultural code—the non-Native one—ignoring the harmonizing and unifying of dual perspectives. In a provocative call for an "ethnocriticism," Krupat has adopted a critical stance that attempts "to alter or ambiguate Western narrative and explanatory categories. . . . To practice ethnocriticism, at any rate, will require real engagement with the epistemological and explanatory categories of Others, most particularly as these animate and propel other narratives. The necessary sorts of movement, therefore, are not only those between dominant Western paradigms but also those between Western paradigms and the as-yet-to-be-named paradigms of the Rest" (*Ethnocriticism* 113). The limited scholarship Krupat wishes to replace uses accepted Western categories and methods of analysis. If this criticism has an anthropological orientation, it asks questions that essentially boil down to: How Native American is it? Does the narrative fall within accepted preconceptions? Is it consistent with the published literature we have on a certain tribe or with the critic's experience with individual members of a tribal group? If this limited criticism has a sociological orientation, it asks questions concerned with the way Native American society has decayed or how the work criticizes American society and its values. If it has a psychological orientation, it may probe the nature of motivation of character. Or it may adopt what is believed to be a Native perspective as it searches for the key referent in traditional culture such as a specific ritual or oral narrative, which the critic sees as representing the complexity of the text. All of these approaches reinforce the established paths of Western knowledge or a limited notion of Native perspectives. Community, continuity, myth, ritual, and identity can easily be overlooked as the goals of the dominant discourse take over. Dasenbrock observes, "The temptations in studying such bicultural writers is to deny their biculturality, to privilege one of their formative cultures in the name of authenticity or the other in the name of universality. And the temptation is stronger when the cultures are so obviously not fused but still separate and in a state of tension and interaction" (317). The mediational text uses at least two perspectives so that neither is subsumed rather exist in a dynamic confluence that encourages deeper cross-cultural questions in various audiences. An appropriate methodology to study such texts must also use at least two perspectives. A mediational approach might follow the formation of mythic patterns in the story while defining psychic unity, or it might examine ritual meaning developed in a social confrontation.

Leslie Silko's novel *Ceremony* is an example of a richly mediated text. Silko's protagonist, Tayo, grows to an understanding of racism, American education, even nuclear power, as he begins to perceive the world in terms of the struggle in a medicine man's mythic story. Laguna storytelling discourse is juxtaposed against psychological determinations of meaning, and the non-Native world becomes illuminated through Laguna cultural understandings. Conversely, when Silko has Tayo realize that the path back to harmony with the land and

Laguna culture requires that Tayo live again in the multiple present moment and that he must rely on the Laguna language, whose grammar subtly implies a world where the past and future exist linguistically always in the present, she voices a perception of time and linguistic distinctions that do not arise out of traditional Laguna culture. Indeed, fundamental to an appreciation of the novel is the idea that the old ceremonies need to change. Tayo's survival, and thus Laguna's, will rely on the visions of people such as an unorthodox Navajo medicine man and the mixed-blood marginalized Tayo. These elements propose epistemological lessons that the implied Native reader must learn. Ultimately, Silko intimates that non-Native structures like the novel will help to create new ceremonies when the old kiva ceremonies have lost their efficacy. Some elements of Laguna epistemology are being challenged, while others are being reinforced; at the same time the non-Native audience's epistemology is being challenged and satisfied. Familiar methods may be used to reach alien goals or vice versa. Silko's *Ceremony* skillfully mediates this new continent of old pathways.

Gerald Vizenor also uses the potential of mediation to its fullest. In *Bearheart: The Heirship Chronicles*, a novel about a futuristic dystopia where gasoline is scarce, he completely mythologizes the characters, their actions, and the purpose of the book. Actions are linked less with causation than with continuance on a mythic plane, so that events resonate with significance on a number of epistemological planes, both Native and non-Native. On the other hand, Vizenor develops a psychological dimension of essentially mythic characters, though only to subvert his reader's expectations. Stylistically, he pursues narrative strategies similar to other contemporary avant-garde writers in order to present a satirical critique of American society and Native American survival. In other writings, Vizenor achieves a non-Native sociological goal, such as when he analyzes the power structure of a university department through characters at once mythic and realistic.

Vizenor's updated trickster tales place Native American perceptions in a modern framework to delight Native audiences. However, for non-Native audiences, he explains, "I would like to imagine tribal experience for the non-Indian, whose frame of reference is very different from ours" (*Song* 165). Allen emphasizes that this mediational artistic world is one very close to the actual lived experience of contemporary Native Americans, a position intertwined with two cultures and perspectives.[6] In mediating through these differing perspectives, writers try to create patterns that harmonize. They draw on their mediational experience and dual perception of the world to create a mediational discourse. Hayden White outlines the relationship between discourse and experience when he writes, "A discourse is itself a kind of model of the processes of consciousness by which a given area of experience, originally apprehended as simply a field of phenomena demanding understanding, is assimilated by analogy to those areas of experience felt to be *already* understood as to *their* essential natures" (4–5). The mediational experience of the Native American writer is passed on to implied readers as they struggle to bring meaning and psychic unity to the text.

Vizenor has written about mixed-bloods or métis as individuals with great creative potential. He calls them *earthdivers* (characters from tribal creation stories) who bring up small kernels of meaningful cultural sand, blowing on them with their trickster-inspired breath to create new turtle worlds of discourse. He sees this situation as similar to the position of contemporary Native writers. Ultimately, for Vizenor, all Native Americans are métis and all non-Natives are called to follow them:

> Métis earthdivers waver and forbear extinction in two worlds. Métis are the force in the earthdiver metaphor, the tension in the blood and the uncertain word, the imaginative and compassionate trickster on street corners in the cities. When the mixedblood earthdiver summons the white world to dive like the otter and beaver and muskrat in search of earth, and

federal funds, he is both animal and trickster, both white and tribal, the uncertain creator in an urban metaphor based on a creation myth that preceded him in two world views and oral traditions. (*Earthdivers* xvii)

Whether by blood or experience, Native Americans today, especially writers, express a mixed heritage. As old and isolating world views give rise to new ones, the writer acts out his or her role as mediator-creator. The existence of non-Native and Native audiences forces the contemporary Native American writer to evaluate consciously the cultural codes incorporated into the text as well as to evaluate which implied readers are paying attention to which elements in the text. In interviews, Silko has commented on her need to weigh each element of the story in order to decide first which stories can be told effectively and then how much to tell and in what detail. She does not want to lose an outsider by including too much Laguna detail nor a Native American reader by over-emphasizing goals and methods too Western. She consciously analyzes which cultural codes to use and to whom she is speaking at any one point in the text. Louis Owens sees in this balancing a "matrix of incredible heteroglossia and linguistic torsions and an intensely political situation" (*Other* 15).[7] This level of self-reflexiveness can also be seen as generating what Bakhtin would call "two-voiced discourse." Todorov, interpreting Bakhtin, contributes his own gloss: "Two-voiced discourse is characterized by the fact that not only is it represented but it also refers simultaneously to two contexts of enunciation: that of the present enunciation and that of a previous one. Here the author 'can also use the discourse of the other toward his own ends, in such a way that he imprints on this discourse, that already has, and keeps, its own orientation, a new semantic orientation. Such a discourse must, in principle, be perceived as being another's. A single discourse winds up having two semantic orientations, two voices'" (*Bakhtin* 71). Mediation is two-voiced discourse that appropriates one audience's discourse to force its own cognitive reorientation, but it does so in two separate fields of discourse. The ultimate task of the contemporary Native American writer is to find ways to speak to multiple audiences at the same time and at different levels.[8]

Much contemporary anthropological theory has been engaged in a task similar to that of the contemporary Native American writer. There is a movement that concerns itself with how to turn the dominant anthropological discourse into a dialogue with the Other. Clifford, Marcus, Fischer, and others have spearheaded this inquiry, attempting to clarify the lines of cross-cultural interaction. The literary scholar may find it useful to conceive of the world of mediational discourse as akin to Roy Wagner's concept of culture as an invented realm that the anthropologist creates to mediate between the reality of the world of the Other.[9] But more to the point, this mediational and cultural world incorporates the discourse of the Other, but from both conceptions of the Other, both audiences' perceptions. It seems to me that Native American writers successfully complete the task that contemporary anthropology sets out for itself through their creation of "a world, or an understanding of the *differences between* two worlds, that exists between persons who were indeterminately far apart, in all sorts of ways, when they started out on their conversation" (Tedlock 323). Now, however, they have conversed in a new grammar.

2

Multiple Narratives and Story Realities

◆

In discussing the weaknesses of many historical texts dealing with Native American identity, James Clifford writes:

> Stories of cultural contact and change have been structured by a pervasive dichotomy: absorption by the other *or* resistance to the other. A fear of lost identity, a Puritan taboo on mixing beliefs and bodies, hangs over the process. Yet what if identity is conceived not as a boundary to be maintained but as a nexus of relations and transactions actively engaging a subject? The story or stories of interaction must then be more complex, less linear and teleological. (344)

The mediation process creates a text that can promote continuity, and yet at the same time, define identity in the midst of transactions. Each separate cultural conversation engages works to create a volatile, self-reflexive, complex narrative and complex identity. Mediation expresses both traditional Native American cultures and contemporary American culture, engendering a dynamic that structures both the creation of the text and the experience of the reader and becomes the point of origin for contemporary Native American literature. The poles of the dynamic, the wisdom of Native American tradition and that of Western tradition, are fairly familiar. Of course, any such generalizations deal with hundreds of different groups and might ultimately prove to serve Western tradition more than Native American traditions, yet enough commentary has been collected from both tribal and non-tribal sources to make such general differences at least hypothetical. However, their usefulness may be limited merely to leading us in a different direction. The danger is always that difference will be essentialized and the sense of the dialogic lost.

It is a critical and popular commonplace that, to quote Allen, "Indians don't think the way non-Indians do: this distinction is partly one of tribal consciousness as opposed to the consciousness of the urbanized, industrial cultures, but it is also a distinction between new world and old world thought, between systems based on wholeness and those based on division and separation." Traditionally, Native American cultures envision synchronous time as conforming to a circular and holistic view of phenomena, endowing each event with multiple significance. As Allen suggests, their traditional literatures are "achronistic rather than synchronistic" ("American" 1058). Wisdom is accretive, and human interaction with the powers of the universe demanded, emphasizing what Barre Toelken calls "the reciprocal relationships between people and the sacred *processes* going on in the world" ("Seeing" 14). Louis Owens expands on this when he suggests that Native writers present "a way of looking at the world that is new to Western Culture. It is a holistic, ecological perspective, one that places essential value upon the totality of existence, making humanity equal to all elements but superior to none and giving humankind crucial responsibility for the care of the world we inhabit" (*Other* 29). Taken together, these large generalizations direct our attention toward what N. Scott Momaday calls an "Indian worldview" ("Native" 79).[1] Conversely, the Western tradition encourages a more linear view of time, concepts of causality and rationality, immediate practical understandings, and the preeminence of the individual. And for the last few centuries at least, a premium has been placed on the literate at the expense of the oral.

If it is clear that the two groups have differing epistemological systems, it is also true that narrative in each area has differing goals and structures, even though those goals and structures can be altered by time and changing functions. One of the primary characteristics of postmodern writing, as Stephen Tyler describes it, is a focus "on the outer flow of speech, seeking not the thought that 'underlies' speech, but the thought that *is* speech" (45). This focus on the thought-that-is-speech brings contemporary writing into a position to employ an oral perspective and thus find a common mediational ground with Native American literature.

While mediation is encoded into contemporary Native American texts, behind these texts lies the "story," as the Russian formalists were quick to point out. The story (fable) reflects culture and tradition, while the plot (sujet) deals with the mechanisms of patterning. Both of these narrative levels reflect their cultural determinations and their genesis in fields of discourse. When the distinction is expanded by the structuralists to *story*, *recit*, and *narration*, the *recit* takes on a solid reality of words on a page, but also partakes of the content or the world it evokes. But all levels of narrative take their meaning from the story, a cultural construct. Todorov even goes so far as to define the story as the reality evoked (*Poetics* 45). Iser, following A. N. Whitehead, sees narrative events as a paradigm of reality in that they delineate a process. Each real and narrative event represents interacting circumstances of the cultural conversations that are constantly changing. Their shapes establish borders that are constantly being transcended in the continuous process of realizing phenomena that constitute reality. Iser asserts:

> In literature, where the reader is constantly feeding back reactions as he obtains new information, there is just such a

continual process of realization, and so reading itself 'happens' like an event, in the sense that what we read takes on the character of an open-ended situation, at one and the same time concrete and yet fluid. . . . Reading, then, is experienced as something which is happening—and happening is the hallmark of reality. (68)

The narratives or stories establish a palpable reality. Moreover, we can see events as having meaning in a number of fields of discourse simultaneously as well as on a number of levels of reality. These distinctions can be easily appreciated in contemporary Native American literature, where the text evokes multiple realities, multiple stories out of the dynamic of understanding and interpretation that the writer brings to the act of writing. As the various cultural conversations are engaged and furthered, identity is drawn. Don H. Bialostosky comments that dialogic texts are in the process of "conferring identities on their fellows and their communities, even as they receive identities from them" (792). Each identity-oriented sphere of discourse embedded in the text can be understood as what both Native writers and non-Native writers would call a *story*. The story, to be recognized, must express and fulfill a cultural code, evoke an expected reality, and establish a context that sustains identity. In mediational texts, the path to that identity is open to a wide number of variations. Silko writes of the very tangible reality that the mythic stories evoke: "They are all we have, you see, all we have to fight off illness and death. You don't have anything if you don't have the stories" (*Ceremony* 2). It is clear that in contemporary Native American literature the reality evoked is at least twofold, Western and Native; however, it appears that two parallel structural axes generate four distinct potential stories, or identity-producing realities that are embedded in the text.

Traditional Native American oral narratives develop identity in an essentially apsychological manner, a characteristic that Ruth Underhill suggests confuses white readers who expect psychological motivations.[2] Melville Jacobs writes about the appreciation of oral tales: "The important thing to keep in mind is that the narrator did not verbalize actors feelings. The absence of verbalized feelings was so complete that the scholar may only speculate about the actors' and audience's feelings" (5). Actors in a mythic story are defined by what they do, not by how they feel or what their motivation is. In a sense, actors exist in order to enable their characteristics to exist, and the characteristics exist to provide action. Tricksters are foolish and therefore act foolishly. Tricksters act foolishly because they are foolish. The narrative turns Western causality on its head because it remains outside linear time and psychology.

Actors are completely defined by their mythological context, but their identity extends beyond the story. A mythological story will often appear in contemporary Native American writing because it is an important cultural dimension in determining identity and place. For Native American readers, brought up on the oral tradition, myth and everyday reality are often fused and become a single source of knowledge. Anthropologist Richard K. Nelson, in his study of the Koyukon, points out the importance of the mythic spiritual dimension and the wisdom gained in contemporary life from the old stories when he writes, "The natural and supernatural worlds are inseparable; each is intrinsically a part of the other. . . . Explanations for the origin, design, and functioning of nature, and for proper human relationships to it, are to be found in the stories of the Distant Time" (227). Myth is an accepted epistemological reality, and an aid to knowing oneself. Elaine Jahner explains, "There [in Native American communities] the myths are an intimate part of ordinary daily activities, because they tell of the drama that gives meaning to the ordinary." The implied Native reader would be expected to understand identity as it is evoked by a mythic reality, a reality full of spiritual efficacy. Jahner quotes Gyula Ortutay to explain that in Native American communities, myths constitute "a living part of the world of realities; not a tale, but a true living reality, the authenticity of which was not at all inferior to that of real experiences in the tangible world" ("Critical" 214). When this story or evoked reality appears in a contemporary text, a character's identity emerges through the mythological story. The character and the implied readers are then both brought to establish their identities. In the mythological story, "Interpretation becomes not so much an imposition of meaning by readers onto a text as it is exposing their selves to the meaning assigned to them by myth" (Cove 33). Silko, Welch, Vizenor, Momaday, and others present protagonists who learn to look outward to the universe and to tradition, to a dimension that is as immemorial as spirit power, and therein find who they are. This path to identity may be confusing to the implied non-Native reader; as Kay Sands has pointed out in her discussion of Native American autobiography, the Native autobiographer "tends to look outward toward the world rather than inward to the person telling the story; and this focus has an effect beyond understated expression of feeling that may be equally puzzling to non-Native readers—the apparent lack of motivation in the characters in the narrative" ("American" 61). Yet this very experience of the mythic is one of the prime epistemological goals of contemporary Native writers.

The mythic mode of identity production might be considered essentially passive or static because while the protagonist must discover this sense of identity, he or she does not create it. It has existed previous to the act of searching and was perhaps even preordained as an eternal source of identity and place. The mythic sphere of discourse, usually revealed in oral tradition, reveals a mediational stance with little self-reflexiveness. While the mythic story may question its own path toward finding a mythic identity, the defined identity itself is a richly endowed cultural phenomenon existing in a widely known discourse field.

On the other hand, as Allen points out in *The Sacred Hoop,* private psychological motivation seems an alien process, and many Native American cultures seek to encourage an individual to merge his or her being "with that of the community and to know within oneself the communal knowledge of the tribe. In this art, the greater self and the all-that-is are blended into a balanced whole" (*Sacred* 55). An individual is encouraged to find the greater self in the communal and, perhaps, in the smallest and most essential unit of the communal, the family. This path to identity is an active one where the individual works with others to define a place and existence for himself or herself. Silko notes how important the community is to the reality of Native American experience: "The community is tremendously important. That's where a person's identity has to come from, not from racial blood quantum levels" ("Stories" 19). Individuals examine themselves to see how they fit in to the changing tribal web while at the same time the community examines them to see what their role will be.

These apsychological definitions of identity are echoed in the many attempts to define Native American identity on the basis of culture and community, such as in the work of Jack D. Forbes and Geary Hobson.[3] Both scholars emphasize a community-oriented definition of who an Indian is. In commenting on this much recognized phenomenon, Krupat terms it the "collective constitution" of the Native self (*Voice* 134).[4] In this level of narrative, the textual discourse becomes highly self-reflexive, as the characters attempt to examine themselves in terms of how they are perceived by others. The community frequently requires that individuals and thus Native protagonists look at themselves to see how they fit in. They repeatedly examine values and actions against a communal standard and definition of identity. For the sake of argument, we might say that the human need to establish identity can often be satisfied within the Native American world views by two evoked realities or two stories: one outward-looking, immemorial, and static; one inward-looking, immediate, and active. These two stories allow many contemporary Native American writers to satisfy a Native audience's expectations of character identity. When asked whom his audience was, writer Simon Ortiz answered: "Anybody who reads. listens, feels. Anybody, but maybe Indian people particularly since I always try to focus upon the relationships among us all" ("That's" 48).

These two forms of stories or realities that create identity may seem a bit unusual to readers without extensive cross-cultural experience. Accustomed as we are to seeing identity in sociological and psychological terms, those of us brought up with a Western world view have a tendency to project our expectations and epistemology onto other cultures. Clifford Geertz reminds his readers that "the Western conception of the person as a bounded, unique, more or less integrated motivational and cognitive universe, a dynamic center of awareness, emotion, judgement, and action organized into a distinctive whole and set contrastively both against other such wholes and against its social and natural background, is, however incorrigible it may seem to us, a rather peculiar idea within the contexts of the world's cultures" (126). Contemporary Native American writers are drawing on a more holistic vision of the individual, a vision that makes room for different ways of experiencing self and the world around us. Jahner explains, "In the living tribal traditions, many people still have an immediately experienced sense of the ways in which different kinds of narrative have to do with different ways of knowing. With such a perception goes a responsibility for keeping alive the many ways of experiencing and knowing reality" ("Critical" 211). The task for contemporary Native American writers is not just to keep alive these ways of knowing, but to make the implied non-Native reader experience and appreciate them. However, they also strive to move their implied Native reader to Western ways of knowing and to new forms of Native knowing.

The mythic and communal identity-producing narratives exist potentially in any contemporary Native American text. In "American Indian Fiction," Allen discusses a multiple narrative concept, though she does not explain how the stories are generated, except to allude to the ritual importance of the number four in many Native cultures. She gives the possible Native code stories the names of *arcane* and *ceremonial*. The author does not completely explain the distinction and relationship between these two kinds of stories, but she does imply that the ceremonial story is told to aid and complete the arcane story, indeed all the stories. As Mircea Eliade and others have commented, ceremonial stories require the arcane or mythic stories as the patient or listener must be brought into the energy and creativity of the cosmogenic (mythic) story for his rebirth and renewal.[5] Indeed the ceremonial story requires the mythic story to create meaning. In effect, these two stories that Allen identifies are really one. In concluding each test, the character gains an arcane wisdom that places him or her in relation to the mythic and spiritual beings and forces addressed in ceremony. Clearly at the end of Silko's novel *Ceremony*, the protagonist has completed a real and mythic ceremony and, as the two stories intertwine, is given a place and an identity in myth and in the community of priests and elders. The stories complement each other in the different aspects of identity produced: mythic and communal. The protagonist, devoid of characteristics at the beginning, is filled up with the meanings of myth and the values of the community. These mythic and communal stories encompass and extend Allen's categories of the arcane and the ceremonial.

In a discussion of narrative structures, Todorov, drawing upon Jakobson, identifies two essentially different modes of narrative organization. A brief consideration of these modes might further clarify how mediation prepares the ground for two different types of narrative, each of which defines identity according to its own cultural world view. In language, one may at any one moment emphasize a certain linearity and causality, especially in the verb, or one may choose to emphasize the actor or the event, the subject. These possibilities translate into narrative as moments in which the audience wants to know what each event will provoke, what will happen next, or moments in which the audience wants to know what the event is, what is its nature. Todorov calls these narratives of *contiguity* and narratives of *substitution* (*Poetics* 135–36).

In contemporary Native American texts, one can find contiguity expressed in the dual dimensions of narrative identity or substitution in the determination of the significance of event. In an apsychological context, the mythic story presents a thread of horizontal, progressive movement (contiguity) often based on character traits, codes of belief and behavior, and actions completed. In the completion of the story, codes are fulfilled, lessons taught, and worlds righted. In the communal story, each event brings vertical questions about the actor's social situation, relation to family, how others view him, and what he should really do now in relation to the community (substitution). This axis, born out of Native American audience expectations, represents one plane of any implied reader's response to the next. As Native American writers seek to fulfill the expectations of Native audiences and non-Native audiences, they may emphasize and intertwine these stories. By engaging existing discourse fields, they seek to mediate them in such a way as to express Native and non-Native values.

The perception of multiple narratives might be clearer when one looks at the Western pole of the mediation process. Western epistemological codes have always encouraged linearity, nonassociative thinking, and a concept of rationality that rests on a psychological view of character. Still, inside these cultural expectations, one can make a distinction between inward-looking and outward-looking approaches to identity. The bedrock of character in this world view is the inward make-up of the individual, who constitutes a cogni-

tive universe, as Geertz phrases it (126). Contemporary Western audiences define their personal identity primarily
through this psychological understanding, and they expect
fictional characters to do likewise. The psychological story
emphasizes the unique position of the character. Event exists
to reveal character, or as Henry James in "The Art of Fiction"
put it, "What is incident but the illustration of character?
What is either a picture or a novel that is *not* of character?
What else do we seek in it and find in it?" (15–16). A reader is
led not so much to follow the action as to see incident in terms
of personal motivation. In the psychological story, characters
who seek their identity must look inward to reveal a nature
that has always been theirs. They do not create it. Early
developmental experiences imposed a structure that the ma-
ture adult seeks to have revealed to him or her. This essentially passive search creates the substitution narrative of the
psychological story.

Characters may also look outward to society for a definition
of identity. They interact with the society around them and
define themselves according to its norms and their sociological role. They may seek to base their understanding of self on
a unit larger than one being, an understanding of their
position in and conditioning by a group of people. Often, as
in naturalistic or Marxist approaches, identity is forged by the
sum of social forces, which play upon and find expression
through individuals. When characters act, the reader is led to
pay attention to the results of the act, to be more concerned
with what will happen next, rather than to the motivation.
The meaning of the event and a character's identity are found
in the larger context of social forces. This often leads to
cultural conflict in the novel, which may then cause a character to learn something of his or her identity. Allen has
analyzed this as an important aspect of the non-Native's
appreciation of the narrative: "Cultural conflict often is sec-
ondary to the main event, and is incorporated into the stories
because the writer needs to satisfy non-Indian readers who

can and generally will understand the significance of that theme" ("American" 1059). Western audiences validate this form of knowing and identity in their own lives and expect it in fictional constructs of experience. The reality evoked is one in which the character actively participates in roles, expectations and social forces. In this area of discourse we may see the contiguous structure of the sociological story.

To summarize, the two epistemological poles of traditional Western culture and traditional Native American cultures may be used by the contemporary Native American writer to illuminate each other. The text draws on different spheres of discourse to create a new context for meaning and identity. As the text proceeds, it mediates epistemological structures and the writer's self-reflexive interpretations of those structures of meaning and identity. Through a process of misreading and reevaluation of the identity revealed in the stories from each sphere of discourse, readers proceeds to merge with the textual perspectives and alter their perceptions. The implied readers recognize and validate an inward and outward looking understanding of identity but are also positioned to validate differing definitions. Because of the implied readers' and writer's mediation, four possible types of stories are generated: the mythological story, the communal story, the psychological story, and the sociological story. As the text begins, both Native and non-Native implied readers perceive the protagonists as empty, devoid of the meaning and identity that the four stories will eventually create. Of course, not every contemporary Native American fictional text will manifest all four "stories" to equal degrees. Only one or two stories might be emphasized. One story might displace another, or remain in a null position in the set.

When the implied readers complete the text, they have unified the two world views and various narratives, engaging in a number of discourse fields. As such they are capable of appreciating a vision of the world that merges the mythic, communal, sociological, and psychological significance of event. When the implied non-Native readers are placed in this perceptual position, they begin to experience something of Native American world views. Implied Native readers may have this perception renewed and redefined for a contemporary world. Benjamin Lee Whorf explains this perception of the world by reference to a cognitive linguistic realm inclusive of what English calls "present" and "future" as well as "subjective":

> The subjective or manifesting comprises all that we call future, **but not merely this;** it includes equally and indistinguishably all that we call mental—everything that appears or exists in the mind, or, as the Hopi would say prefer to say, in the **heart,** not only the heart of man, but the heart of animals, plants and things, and behind and within all the forms and appearances of nature in the heart of nature, and by implication and extension . . . in the very heart of the Cosmos itself. (124)

From this perspective, events unfold, revealing multiple layers of significance and multiple stories that clarify their connections. This is a world view that Allen describes: the self as a moving event in a universe of dynamic equilibrium. Lipsha Morrissey in *Love Medicine*, Tayo in *Ceremony*, and many other characters embrace the mystery of the world, but that mystery exists in a world and world view where knowledge, meaning, truth, and signification already exist in a nontangible realm, which Whorf calls "manifesting," as opposed to the tangible realm where the processes of the world have already been realized as "manifested." These characters perceive the world not as changing or progressing, but as constantly in the process of becoming what it always was, though we could not see it; they see meaning in their lives and in the world revealing itself, manifesting what has always been there. Whorf sees the perception of a "manifesting" world as basic to Native American world view, a world view where the universe is "the striving of purposeful desire, intelligent in character, toward manifestation" (124). Robin

Ridington clarifies Whorf's intentions and insights when he writes, "Whorf's observations about Hopi time could apply equally well to many of other native cultures of North America. . . . Although the Hopi have their own distinctive ceremonies and traditions, these arise out of a more general Indian thought world, which recognizes a timeless, vital or mythic principle in the universe" (22). Contemporary Native American writers shift the epistemological perspective of both implied readers so as to encourage a rejuvenated Native American sense of the creation of meaning and knowledge, one which values the manifesting over the manifested.

An understanding of the nature of multiple narratives should deepen readers' insights into contemporary Native American literature and, ultimately, their appreciation of it. Through mediation and multiple narrative, the contemporary Native American text labors to achieve Bakhtin's "overcoming of otherness" since the text exists in the perspectives of the two worlds facing it.

Intricate Patterns of the Universe

House Made of Dawn

◆

When N. Scott Momaday's *House Made of Dawn* won the Pulitzer Prize in 1969, contemporary Native American Literature was ushered into the literary spotlight. Most reviewers and readers saw clearly that the novel fit into modernist literary tradition in much of its style and content.[1] Yet while praising the novel for its experimental form and sociological content, some reviewers expressed discontent with it.[2] They knew that something outside the classical arc of the tragic hero was happening in the novel, but unwilling to trust the new perceptions required by the novel, a few critics felt an incompleteness, a nonspecificity, and chalked it up to poor writing. Perhaps they understood that Momaday was attempting nothing less than an appropriation of the dominant literary discourse field with the aim of decentering it. As Owens observes, this introduction of a Native American discourse about identity and community had neocolonial implications they did not wish to explore. For beyond the surface sociopolitical narrative, Momaday's text was, indeed, informed by a "profound awareness of conflicting epistemololgies" (*Other* 92). For most readers in 1968, *House Made of Dawn* was the first novel they had ever read by an American

Indian and their expectations of despair, inarticulateness, and closeness to nature were satisfied by Abel, the Indian protagonist of the novel, if not by Momaday. What they also got was an act of literary mediation, which previous Native American texts did not prepare them for, but which moved many readers into new experiences of the world and new perceptions.

Indeed, Momaday does privilege Native American discourse in the book, starting with the most basic and essential element of discourse, the word, and more precisely the spoken word. Momaday believes that the oral tradition and the written tradition are equal in force, function, and value: a position not common in Western literary thought. His use of words from Pueblo storytelling tradition to frame the book and his use of the Navajo Night Chant are only two foregrounded incidents of oral discourse; however, we could easily include his use of Indian humor, oral structuring devices such as repetition, and even oral plot development. For Momaday the storyteller and the writer are natural allies; they "share the same qualities . . . [and are] engaged in pretty much the same activity" (Bruchac 93). Once the distinctions that separate oral literature from written literature are banished, new fields of discourse increase the possibilities of mediation, of new insight, and of experiencing new world views. Consequently a new set of goals and loyalties emerge, which require a shift in perspective from both implied Native and non-Native readers. Momaday remarks, "Yes, I think that my work proceeds from the American Indian oral tradition and carries it along. And vice versa. . . . My purpose is to carry on what was begun a long time ago; there's no end to it that I can see" (qtd. in Coltelli 187). The implied Native readers might be more ready to assume an oral perspective once they see that the ways in which Momaday applies Native oral discourse are both traditional and contemporary. For them, it will be paradoxical to find such oral and communal discourse continued in writing and in the whirlwind of modernist fiction and alienation at that. The implied non-Native reader, encouraged by the modernist style, will easily search for meaning, but will be ushered onto an unfamiliar plane, an oral one, or even a mythic one, thereby being led to assume a perspective closer to an oral Native epistemology.

Oral discourse informs every level of *House Made Of Dawn*. The sense of competing voices in the novels initiates both readers' search for meaning, but it is a search where each voice must be examined and evaluated for its contribution to understanding. In essence, the text reflects a conversation about Abel, Native America, and contemporary existence. The idea-position of each voice reveals only part of the puzzle. As Vizenor suggests, tribal discourse is "more dis-course," a language game that defies simple colonial and social science categorization as well as simple attempts at finding closure of meaning ("Postmodern" 4). Momaday stra-tegically foregrounds chants, peyote religion discourse, myths, memories, and oral history, and lets them interrogate journals, legal language, history, and slogans of modern existence until each field sees its discourse as without hege-mony and as a translation of language of the Other. I would call this confluence the oral form of the novel. Momaday might have had the same concept in mind when he com-mented, "The novel reflects a kind of shape that is real in the American Indian world," a world distinctly oral (qtd. in Coltelli 92). Or, as Kenneth Rosen has suggested, comment-ing on some of the oral elemens, "Facts, lore, and legend are so carefully interwoven in this work that the form becomes the content, the manner itself is clearly one of the most important aspects of the novel's message" (58).

Still other levels of the novel reflect various aspects of oral discourse. Momaday's style itself reveals an oral foundation.[3] Allen contends that the achronological structure of the novel derives more from Momaday's use of oral, tribal time than from the traditions of the psychological novel that might substitute subjective time for objective. *House Made of Dawn's* "accretative" nature breaks down the distinctions between real and surreal, between fact and dream, and is reflective of "the integrative nature of ritual consciousness" (*Sacred* 94). For Allen, the structures of tribal male ritual life are the essential devices to be identified: "The plot loosely follows a conflict-crisis-resolution pattern, but the novel is more deeply structured to match the Navajo ceremonials known as chantways" (88). Linda Hogan further points out Momaday's use of oral patterns, such as accumulation and release, and repetition, to stimulate the visual imagination. She writes:

> These methods are characteristic of oral tradition, in which the word and the object are equal and in which all things are united and in flux. The distinctions between inner and outer break down. Momaday, making use of these oral techniques in his poetic language, returns Abel, along with the reader, to an earlier time "before the abyss had opened between things and their names."
>
> This return gives to words a new substance and power not unlike that of oral ritual. The life of the word and the fusion of the words and object, by means of the visual imagination, return the participant or reader to an original source that is mythic, where something spoken stands for what is spoken about and there is "no difference between the telling and that which is told." (175–76)

For much of the novel, Momaday allows these oral and ritual elements to remain backgrounded, only occasionally highlighting them in the text. His mediation is not in eliminating the psychological underpinnings of the modern novel but in finding a way to make them serve Native purposes. The foregrounded sense of stream of consciousness and monologue are slowly recontextualized, even defamiliarized, so that a shift of perspective is required if the non-Native implied reader is to follow the role assigned to him or her. The Native implied reader is led to discover that written discourse can nurture and extend the field of oral discourse. The embedded oral discourse begins to influence the sense of style, plot, and character of the implied non-Native reader so that a new world view and sense of time are revealed. The non-Native reader's uncertainty and confusion can only be resolved when he or she decides to pay attention to the new discourse context and establish a new meaning for chanting, running, and return. The Native reader is guided to see through the psycho-social turmoil to find the mythic pattern beneath the flux of modern existence.

As the text of the novel draws upon oral discourse, it introduces a tribal world view that Allen calls ritual and Hogan calls mythic. Both readers are led to a larger, timeless plane connected to all that is around us and on which ultimate meaning rests. This mythic perception is required to appreciate how Abel, Francisco, and the Pueblo people are connected to the natural world and to the eternal struggle between good and evil. Mircea Eliade has observed that for the believer, "Myth teaches him the primordial 'stories' that have constituted him existentially; and everything connected with his existence and his legitimate mode of existence in the Cosmos concerns him directly" (*Myth and Reality* 12). Owens argues that the opening passages of the novel, which describe the landscape and present the image of Abel running, create a timeless, mythic background against which Olguin, Angela, Tosamah, Benally, and the albino, emerge (*Other* 93–96).[4] Abel must learn to return to the stories and to connection with the cosmos. The non-Native reader, for whom the journey is new, follows him along. The Native reader is not merely assured that tradition is correct, but that struggle and mediation are also required to renew a mythic world view. Abel and both readers are shown the need to bring mythic time into our mundane perceptions of the world around us. Eliade reminds us that in this process the participant's sense of time is fundamentally altered: "By 'living' the myths one emerges from profane, chronological time and enters a time that is of a different quality, a 'sacred' Time at once primordial and indefinitely recoverable" (*Myth and Reality* 18). For Momaday this act of imagination is not only necessary for wholeness, but is the essence of a person's existence.[5] Through imagination, especially literary imagination, that person bridges the gap between "us and that which is apart from us" (*Ancestral* 206). Only such an imaginative shift to mythic time and mythic meanings can bring Abel, the readers, and modern society back to primordial unity and eliminate what Momaday sees as the "psychic dislocation of ourselves in time and space" ("Man" 166).

It is this dimension of the novel that people have characterized as having a healing effect. Such healing requires a profound imaginative act from the non-Native reader, one which Momaday evokes with subtle poetic and religious imagery. The most extensive discussion of Momaday's use of mythic discourse to date has been in Susan Scarberry-Garcia's book *Landmarks of Healing*.[6] She analyzes the Pueblo, Kiowa, and especially Navajo structures, themes, and symbols to outline the "healing patterns that Momaday has embedded in this new story" (2). She finds extensive evidence of patterning similar to Navajo chants, whose function is to heal an individual who is out of harmony with the sacred processes of the world. The chants reestablish the patient in the mythic world. After a discussion of this process, she concludes:

> Momaday's method of text-building is parallel to the healing experience. The novelist creates a powerful unified story by overlapping multiple, seemingly fragmented, narratives. Using the techniques of parallelism, circularity, and repetition from oral tradition, Momaday presents sacred songs and stories as models of the process of composition and reassemblage of inner energies.
>
> Whereas the Twins and the bears are the central images in the novel that make the healing process cohere, the dense complicated storysherd structure of the novel forces the reader to think imaginatively and to associate parts of the story holistically. This act of consciously seeking relationships in

order to create a whole meaningful story is parallel to, or even contiguous with, the healing process. To recognize that the powers of the natural world and of Native American Literature are inseparable is to unite the sources of healing in the land with the intrinsic healing power in *House Made of Dawn*. (16)

The non-Native's imaginative act of allowing the new form of the old stories to establish context and meaning brings him or her back to the power of the word and heals the split between "us and that which is apart from us." However, the Native reader must also accept the potential for healing that a non-oral object like a novel can bring. Such a perspective requires a movement away from the idea of healing rituals as fixed in cultural tradition. Sections of the novel, such as the lectures of Tosamah, which range so freely through Western and Native traditions, provide highly mediated discourse that can inform both implied readers about the creative power of the word, while evoking images of the trickster in Native readers and images of the social critic in non-Native audiences. With Abel's return to community and ritual, the implied Native reader might be placed in the literary ritual in which the protagonist is cured of what Vizenor has termed "cultural schizophrenia" (Crossbloods 149). The implied Native readers then become participants in a new ritual aimed at curing whatever cultural schizophrenia they may feel, if only that induced by the novel. When both readers participate in the new/old myth, they experience, in Eliade's words, a "sudden breakthrough of the sacred that really *establishes* the World and makes it what it is today." This world of myth, even in the novel, can become "the exemplary model for all significant human activity" (*Myth and Reality* 6). The ritual participant, Abel, and reader are then placed back at the distant time of origin, when harmony and balance were established, and they are then ready to appreciate creative power.

This may prove to be a difficult breakthrough for some non-Native readers. Even Scarberry-Garcia acknowledges that the healing is "a largely 'invisible' dimension in the novel. . . . In order to be able to read the difficult religious levels of the text, which voice in symbolic language the relationship between person, place and healing powers, it is necessary to comprehend the culturally distinct Native American belief systems that underlie the composition of the novel" (4). Native metaphysics and epistemology structure the deep and conclusive meanings in the novel, and the implied non-Native readers will need to move toward a validation of Pueblo and Navajo world view. However, the movement of the non-Native readers toward that world view is beneficial for them and the future of cross-cultural interactions.

The mythic bedrock of the novel is available to both audiences. The contemporary decay and confusion of some Native people does not negate the harmonious balance of spirit world and physical world that creates the essential nature of existence in the Indian world. Though Momaday is writing about what he calls "a tragic generation" (qtd. in Coltelli 94), he wants his readers, especially his non-Native readers, to realize that "the Indian has an understanding of the physical world and of the earth as a spiritual entity that is his, very much his own. The non-Indian can benefit a good deal by having that perception revealed to him" (qtd. in Bruchac 190). What must be revealed is that Indians, like the people Momaday knew as he was growing up in Jemez, "understood the intricate patterns of the universe. In the Indian world, an understanding of order is paramount." (*Ancestral* 170). The novel is patterned not just to present a static picture of this understanding of order but to make readers experience it. However, that order is backgrounded for most of the novel and must be arrived at through restructured perceptions.

This shift in the non-Indian reader's perception is not unlike the distinction between *manifesting* and *manifested* described by Whorf. The novel's breakdown of chronology and causation opens up a textual standpoint where a mythic sense of meaning can emerge, where time and place switch relationships, where Western world view gives way to Native world view. In what Whorf describes as the Hopi concept of subjective experience, mental and mythic levels of experience become more important in determining meaning than the objective or psychical levels. Martha Trimble observes that the disorientation of the reader results from a lack of standard motivation in character and standard causation in plot.[7] But the disorientation stems from a more essential shift. The new standpoint guides both implied readers from an opposition between what the readers think they know and what they really do know, to a more essential epistemological perception of myth. However, this evolving position allows the reader some freedom to explore the relation of physical detail to the sociological and psychological levels of the novel. Trimble concludes that the major opposition generating the text is between Native world view and Western world view: "At least with reference to the book, if the contrasts between actual knowledge and apparent knowledge can be reconciled, it will be clear that the materials Momaday presents have not been merely organized into unity by the artistic conventions available for the purpose but rather have become fused into unity through the combined efforts of both the author and reader. These efforts might eventually yield cultural results also" (21). Trimble decides that the mediational mix of the text, its inclusion of Native discourse on religion, myth and culture with more accessible stories such as those of returned World War II veterans, holds the non-Indian reader back, leaving him or her with "an abiding sense of what he does not know" (24). However, more to the point is that the reader is held off from making familiar conclusions about the psychology and sociology of Abel and his community. Both implied readers move from surface text about confusion and disarray to subtext of order and pattern. Andrew Wiget notes, "Structurally, Momaday wove complex strands of tribal mythic reference as subtext throughout the tapestry of his fiction, rather than blatantly alternate text and pre-text. The result is a more challenging, but also more satisfying experience for the reader, who, as Scarberry-Garcia rightly points out, is, like the novel's protagonist Abel, healed by the recognition of the mythic patterning, the significance, of the apparently mute, idiosyncratic historical moment" (Foreword xiii–xiv).

Yet surely the historical moment of the novel may not be as mute or idiosyncratic as some critics present it. The background requires a foreground in the gestalt of perception before their values can be switched. Certainly the historical moment has been the focus of many critics and readers of the novel, perhaps as many as those who have focused on the mythic superstructure. Many critics have concentrated on Momaday's apparent commentary on the status of Native Americans in modern American society and social and psychological disorientation.[8]

An appreciation of the contemporary social discourse field, however, is essential to understanding the dialogic nature of his text and his mediational pattern. Momaday expects the implied non-Native reader to be shocked a bit by Abel's state and by extension the situation of the contemporary American Indian. Disorientation due to pressure to acculturate is emphasized in the first three parts of the novel. While the non-Native reader may be liberal enough to feel a sense of social injustice, he or she will not automatically be able to participate in the cultural conversation surrounding relocation and termination concepts and language. The implied non-Native reader would most likely first be a little surprised at the continuance of any Native culture, in contrast to the popular stereotype of the disappearing Indian, and second, even if vaguely familiar with the Ira Hayes affair, would attempt to place the text in a larger field of American cultural discourse about acculturation, land theft, social decay, and minority rights, issues foregrounded in the 1960s. He or she would not have immediate access to a conversation about federal Indian policy of the fifties. The real news for this reader is that Native beliefs still exist and that only they account for Abel's behavior and for definitive meaning in the novel. This revelation holds the implied non-Native reader back from a belief that inserting the discourse of the text into the larger American cultural discourse will reveal meaning in the work. The reader may suspect perhaps that modern society has lost a totalizing perspective toward the land and the cosmos and may become encouraged to move toward validation of a Native world view.[9] From this new perspective, that reader can follow Momaday's argument that the disorientation is less a social problem than a spiritual one. He writes thus of the cultural losses experienced by Native peoples: "But the loss is less important to me than the spirit which informs the remembrance, the spirit that informs the pageantry across all ages and which persists in the imagination of every man everywhere" (qtd. in Bruchac 183).

The implied Native reader would see a more specific idea-position in a continuing cultural discussion about relocation and termination policies. He or she would agree about the disastrous nature of the policy and easily appreciate the irony in Benally's appropriation of relocation rhetoric and Tosa-mah's progressive appraisals of Abel's experience. This reader would know damaged individuals from the "tragic generation," yet that would be an old topic, close to closure. The political discourse of the early and mid-sixties often saw the returning veterans assuming leadership roles in tribal communities and demanding changes. On the Navajo reservation that Momaday knows so well, the code talkers and other veterans were demanding better schools, more favorable negotiations with the mines, and new political influence for the tribe on the state level. The contemporary cultural conversation of most tribal groups was not on World War II, but on Vietnam, not on relocation but on the war on poverty and the move toward self-determination initiated by the Kennedy administration. Projects for the Office of Economic Opportunity (OEO), Head Start, political reorganization, and community school initiatives dominated the discourse.

One might be tempted to assert that Momaday's literary discourse exists outside of the context of that conversation, striving for a universalism, but to do so would be to ignore Momaday's use of the discourse field of contemporary Native experience and what he has to say to a Native reader. Clearly the text explores the experiences of the World War II generation that are at the center of sixties Native discourse. As such, it explores something of the motivation of those relatives and friends who accepted relocation and may have even stayed in the cities through the sixties, but it also explores the dislocation of the "tragic generation," giving voice to some of the motivation behind their return to their communities and probing why the perspectives of the World War II generation may differ from the older and the younger generations. By encouraging understanding and maybe even respect for those of the World War II generation, the text would encourage support for their progressive positions. For Momaday, as long as those positions took a larger, longer view of man and woman's relations to the land and to themselves, any changes labeled as progressive might be placed into the category of "a long outwaiting" (58), a process that involves adopting the surface of the dominant society to allow the Native one below the surface to survive.

Certain sections of the text address two different discourse fields, evoking differing meaning in different readers. One good example of how Momaday creates such mediation is in the character of Tosamah. The implied Native reader would immediately see his character informed by the figure of the trickster, important in many Native oral traditions. The trickster's function is to entertain as well as teach and create change. Tosamah does all of these things. Momaday intended the book to engage a specific field of Native discourse called *Indian humor* though few critics have mentioned this. Certainly the teasing and punning associated with Tosamah are characteristic of Indian humor.[10] The playing with words associated with "the whole court business" evoke the field of

Indian humor (*Ancestral* 32). As Vine Deloria Jr., aptly observes, "The more desperate the problem, the more humor is directed to describe it" (147). More specifically, Momaday has commented that he thought Indians would find Tosamah's language play humorous, especially his 1950s Beat description of Abel's trial and his "longhair" experience with the dominant society (*Ancestral* 32). Momaday, of course, intended these sections to be revealing as well as entertaining, yet they may reveal more about the cruel though expected methods of the urban trickster than any truth about Abel. This method of trickster instruction is often called *negative demonstration*. The implied Native might appreciate Tosamah's discussion of the power of the word, but also note that he violates the very truth he would preach. Tosamah's preaching for progressive attitudes presupposes that connections to land and community have been severed. Since implied non-Native readers have been distanced from identification with Tosamah, their attitudes undercut any idea-position in the contemporary cultural conversation that ignores such timeless values. Momaday may support progress, but not without spirit.

As years of critical commentary on the novel have shown, an implied non-Native reader would not readily participate in the humor of the courtroom scene nor in Tosamah's description of Abel's behavior. Moreover, this reader's pursuit of meaning is no less complex, no less mediational than that of the Native reader. While Tosamah voices what appears to be a progressive, proacculturation position, he has attacked the dominant society. He is a kind of Christian, but he takes peyote and encourages a Native sense of community. He lives in Los Angeles but is a descendent of a "lordly and dangerous society of fighters and thieves, hunters and priests of the sun" (129), who believe in the sacredness of the word. He is a walking bag of contradictions, alien enough to hold the non-Native reader off from identifying him. While most non-Native readers may be tempted to adopt something of his progressive approach to the Indian, they cannot let Tosamah speak for them. They are guided to question what is wrong with his position. Why does it not clarify Abel's life and experience? Why does it not help? The implied non-Native reader must mediate and accept a new perspective. He cannot mouth the clichés of progress, but rather, rising from a culturally limited, sociological perspective, he looks to connection, healing, and ritual for meaning.

Nonetheless, some aspects of the novel enter the popular political conversation of the dominant society during the sixties. Most critics agree that Momaday intended to demonstrate that for Abel to be healed and placed in harmony with land and community, he must realize that he cannot overcome evil, either on his own or through confrontation with others. As Allen notes, Abel's violence is symptomatic of his sick spiritual state. It "characterizes him as psychologically disturbed among a people who do not condone interpersonal violence as a means of resolving difficulties"[11] (*Sacred* 88). Of course, while young Momaday was coming to maturity in the post World War II 1950s, the United States was locked in a cold war with the evil empire of communism. A Native world view that balanced good and evil was clearly contrary to the world view that led to the Korean war and produced the arms race. The philosophy of mutually assured destruction predominated over hopes for peaceful coexistence. The world was perceived to be threatened by evil all around, much the same environment that Momaday created for Abel: "a violent world, a world of witchcraft, a world by which he is threatened. Threatened not only psychologically, but physically as well" (*Ancestral* 127). While the "good" violence of World War II may have defeated Germany, Italy, and Japan, it did nothing to answer definitively Western man's question about evil and its place in the world. Momaday introjects Native world view into the dominant society's cultural conversation by moving Abel back toward Pueblo world view. After the cold war of the fifties came a decade of political assassinations and the Vietnam war. All this lashing out against evil on personal and social levels provides a specific context for Momaday's philosophical and religious positions on the big evils of the day. When Abel returns from World War II, a non-Native reader cannot help but think about the parallels between this war's veterans and veterans of the Vietnam War. Consequently, it is important to appreciate that the text takes a position in a specific cultural conversation. As Momaday pointedly remarked about this novel: "I meant to demonstrate some of the natural consequences of war"[12] (*Ancestral* 123).

One character in the novel who reveals a sane attitude toward evil and a path away from destruction is Francisco. Many critics find in him a model of the unity of two worlds that Abel must imitate before he is whole.[13] This unity between cultures and world views, however, is better demonstrated by the narrator or implied author of the text, for his voice and structuring are what allow the various discourses to harmonize and are what restructures both readers' epistemological positions. He is the one who comments on the harmony of the land and the people (5), the natural order (55), the survival of the Pueblo world (58), and on the white trial and the words that dispose of Abel (102). The implied author is the one who can negotiate the various discourse fields and work toward meaning. His perspective is the one constant in the variety of voices and idea-positions, yet he does not tell us what to think and believe about the characters. He allows Tosamah, Olguin, Angela, Benally, Milly, and Francisco to speak for themselves, and the readers draw their own conclusions from their words and actions. Just as Abel must become like Francisco to be healed, both the Native and non-Native reader must become like the implied author to be healed of their modern dislocation, their culture-locked perspectives. As he merges discourse fields, oral and written, mythic and political, and conducts our encounter with various perceptions to reflect something "real in the American Indian world," he establishes a dialogic interaction that requires self-reflexive responses on the part of the readers.[14]

However important for the novel and the reader this exceptional implied author ultimately proves to be, it is Abel who focuses the readers' attention. Abel's plight, his disorientation, becomes the cenral focus for the multiple narratives of identity. The question of Native identity has been extensively discussed in the critical literature surrounding *House Made of Dawn*. Louis Owens determines that in Momaday's work "the question of identity . . . becomes an obsession" (*Other* 92). Matthias Schubnell is also concerned with how the novel explores identity formation, but his focus is on the social and psychological forces at work in "the continual reassessment of their identities" in actual contemporary Native communities as well as in those in the novel. He writes that *House Made of Dawn* "is a novel about an individual and a communal search for identity" (103).

Yet it is Abel's experience, not Walatowa's, that is foregrounded, because part of Momaday's mediational goal is to demonstrate for both implied readers how Western definitions of identity based on psychological and social criteria are too restrictive and incapable of explaining, much less defining, Native identity. The novel begins with Abel confused, in the grips of what appears to be a nervous breakdown. Partly because of his personal background and partly because of his war experiences, he is devastated in Walatowa Pueblo and in Los Angeles. He loses whatever clear sense of identity he had as a young man. And as judged by the standards of the dominant society, Abel fails to achieve a normal life. While Abel's psychic state holds our attention, little psychological motivation is given for his actions and little told of his war experiences. In the psychological story, the non-Native reader sees him increasingly unable to function until he appears as a shattered self in the hospital. Abel's actions in the final scenes come suddenly with no psychological development. A Native reader might see some hope in the final reconciliation with family, the mere act of returning to the community, and certainly the performance of ritual in the burial of Francisco.

However, in terms of a psychological narrative of identity, the final scenes are enigmatic at best, since no clear motivation is given. Yet, this standpoint, where readers attempt to construct psychological identity, is necessary if the non-Native reader is to re-create what he or she constitutes as the reality of identity.

The sociological story provides the most popular path into the novel. Here the outsider, the returned war veteran, fails to adjust to a normal life and relationships as defined by the dominant non-Native society. Every relationship he attempts breaks down. His alcoholism combines with acute alienation from the dominant society and his past to keep him from feeling comfortable in either Native or non-Native society. He is torn between two worlds and defeated by the social forces that push him to war, to jail, and to relocation in the city. He cannot and does not wish to measure up to the dominant society's definition of who he is, and he does not know what his social role in Walatowa is. In terms of the sociological story, he becomes more passive and defeated by the forces of society. Both implied readers are exposed to a variety of social stances in the non-Native and Native worlds, most of which are flawed and undesirable. His final act of joining the dawn runners is not clearly developed in sociological terms, but it may be interpreted as a rejection of modern, dominant society and a search for identity in a smaller group, even though the group has not asked this of him. His active reaching out seems to negate the destructive forces that have toyed with him up until his grandfather's death, unless, as Charles Larson does, one interprets this act as a gesture of suicide (91–92). Non-Native readers who focus only on the psychological and sociological stories might be tempted to agree with Larson that Abel's return expresses only futility and pessimism. However, throughout the text Momaday has been educating the non-Native implied reader to perceive in a new way, a more Native way, the meaning of the experiences described. Momaday anticipates his non-Native audience's expectation of psychological and sociological stories, and while providing narratives on those levels, he skillfully keeps the implied reader away from believing that these are the only or the key stories. The ambiguity is created by embedding the communal and mythic stories in the text, especially in the last section where these other stories become foregrounded. A Native reader may appreciate more completely these other stories of identity even if they are backgrounded at many points in the novel. The use of Jemez storytelling words and many other elements from oral tradition would clue a Native reader into the underlying mythic framework for the text. The dawn runners provide a specific role for Abel to play. In this foot race, the runners experience a mythic confrontation with evil. The narrator relates:

> They were whole and indispensable in what they did; everything in creation referred to them. Because of them, perspective, proportion, design in the universe. Meaning because of them. They ran with great dignity and calm, not in the hope of anything, but hopelessly, neither in fear nor in hatred nor despair of evil, but simply in the recognition and with respect. Evil was. Evil was abroad in the night; they must venture out to the confrontation. (103–104)

Runners are common in Jemez myth and cultural tradition, for running is a ceremonial activity necessary for continuity and harmony.[15] Of Jemez running, Momaday has observed, "To watch those runners is to know that they draw with every step some elemental power which resides at the core of the earth and which, for all our civilized ways, is lost upon those of us who have lost the art of going with the flow of things. In the tempo of that race there is time to ponder morality and demoralization, hungry wolves and falling stars" ("Morality" 40). In the mythic story, Abel is a lost runner out of context, who must confront the reality of evil in the world, whether it is the impersonal evil of war, the corrupt violence of the cop Martinez, or his own personal violence when he kills the albino. A Native reader might be quicker to assign to Abel the mythic identity of a dawn runner. As an individual runner, Abel must experience demoralization and relearn morality, which he does from the dying Francisco. However, his is also the mythic runner's experience. Abel must come to see the necessity of confronting evil on the mythic level just as the other runners do. As he does so, the mythic runner in him emerges from the psychological runner in him through the process of ritual impersonation common in Native religions. As an individual runner, he was confused about his mythic role and consequently his identity. When he joins the other runners and achieves a holistic identity, he becomes less confused about his personal confrontation with evil. The pain and evil he has faced have the same perspective and proportion that the runners' pain does. As he joins the ceremony and feels a song start to come, he draws power from every step. He begins to learn to go with the flow and balance good and evil, pleasure and pain. He has an identity, a mythic identity, which readily fulfills Native expectations but also gives meaning to a non-Native sense of identity. The psychological narrative of identity is completed by the mythic story. Momaday mediates by embedding non-Native psychological elements in a Native mythic story. When the mythic story displaces the psychological story at the end, both audiences are encouraged to examine their epistemological frameworks for limitations, connections, and new insights.

A similar process affects the novel's communal story. The story presents Abel as isolated from his community and from his family, both embodied for him by his grandfather Francisco. As a young man, he began to move into the community and understand himself according to the community's definitions. However, his understanding was partial and tainted by his family's social position. He was unable to harmonize the contradictions and find a place in two worlds as his grandfather did. In her own efforts to find such a place, his mother seems to have been destroyed, and so he moves both spiritually and physically away from the community. Consequently, he is unable to define his identity in terms of the community, and much of the novel presents Abel as being adrift in the flow of social forces that constitute the sociological story of identity. After absorbing what he can of the lessons of community and identity from Benally and others (often by negative demonstration), he returns, and his grandfather's far-ranging, death-bed monologues help Abel begin to understand. The communal story displaces the sociological. Francisco reveals how he was able to harmonize the cultural and communal conflict and still hold on to a clearly defined position among the people of Walatowa. As he speaks of his various initiations, achievements, and communal roles, he reveals an identity actively creating itself in communal terms. After his grandfather dies, Abel prepares him for burial and goes on the dawn run for strength, revitalization, and harmony. The older runner dies and the new runner takes his communal place. From his despairing lack of definition, he has taken an active first step toward an interaction with the community and a communal identity. Momaday mediates again as the communal story completes, modifies, and redefines the sociological story.

With an eye on the multiple narratives foregrounded in the final part of the text, one can see the ritual negate the suicidal, the spirit infuse the body, the self find identity rather than destruction. Ultimately, Momaday reveals the continuance of Native cultures and world view, their wonder and wisdom, as well as the triumph of the human spirit in Abel.

That Other Distance

Winter in the Blood

◆

The nameless narrator in James Welch's *Winter in the Blood* presents a stark image of a contemporary Native American cut off from much of what could sustain and enrich him. His alienation, often the subject of critical discussion, isolates him not only from family and culture, but also from the deepest parts of himself. As Welch explains it, he is caught in a "vision of alienation and purposelessness, aimlessness" (qtd. in McFarland 9).[1] Through a series of episodic encounters with the familiar boundaries of his world, the narrator takes a few small steps toward eliminating the distance he feels from the experiences of the past and the present. He generates some thaw in the winter in his blood.[2]

Through his depiction of how the narrator comes to grips with difficulties, Welch engages his implied Native and non-Native readers in a mediational text designed to encourage the restructuring of non-Native cognitive patterns of interpretation. The novel reinforces Native attitudes toward survival while guiding the Native reader toward a psychological analysis of the political and cultural miasma. The question of identity is then addressed in a manner that challenges non-Native epistemological assumptions and negates stereotypes.

An appreciation of the some of the formal elements through which Welch achieves these mediational goals comes from an examination of the threads of Native and non-Native discourse fields which, though tangled, run throughout the text. Much of the narrator's dialogue and interior monologue grapple with this disrupted discourse; consequently, he is effectively blocked from placing himself in the flow of discourses that could define his identity. Ultimately it is his reconnections with the various discourse fields and their completed narratives as well as with Native epistemology that give the narrator some hope for wholeness. Welch uses this movement through disruptive discourse toward narrative unity to keep the implied reader reading and misreading. The reader actively searches for those connections that the unnamed narrator, until near the end of the novel, appears to avoid.

As Sands suggests, this disrupted field of discourse is foregrounded in the early sections of the novel to intensify the alienation and merge form and content ("Alienation" 97–99). It is clear that the narrator is alienated from his family and the stories they tell about what happened in the past, what they did, and thus who they are. While the grandmother has told the narrator of her early life, she is now silent, especially about the parentage of her daughter (33–38). As disruptive as the silence and veiled hints about Teresa's birth, are the conflicting stories told by those around him. Lame Bull insists that the narrator was a baby when the flood covered the land, but the narrator says he was twenty (8). The stories about who killed the turkey and Amos are all confused (18–19), and all of these stories are tangled with the story of First Raise's death and why he stayed away. The narrator lies about the Cree girl, both to others and to himself. And, of course, the repressed memory, the story of Mose's death, is too devastating for the narrator to remember. His life appears to be composed of stories that are confused. All the discourse that might fix an identity in the family, the land, and the past is incomplete or contradictory.

The stories of other characters, which might have helped the narrator define his relationship to the world around him, are also disrupted. The barmaid from Malta and the airplane man's stories stretch narrative coherence beyond its limit. Marlene and Malvina's stories are all incomplete and confusing as are all the barroom stories. His grandmother's story about her youth is coherent though incomplete, and she has stopped talking. The narrator's dream is the mixing of all the disrupted narratives. What could be dialogic discourse throughout the early part of the novel, with various voices speaking, taking positions, defining meaning in a vibrant cultural dynamic, is disrupted and incomplete. Only with the start of part three does the narrative congeal and the conversation *of* the characters become coherent.

Donald Bialostosky, following Bakhtin, discusses how dialogic discourse shapes narrative and identity. He employs the concept of a dialogic conversation, which exists in a cultural context, to help his audience picture the discourse field that a text engages. Such a field establishes positions and ideas in relation to cultural values and contemporary realities. In his discussion, he underscores the identity-creating function of dialogic conversation when he writes: "Those who take their turns speaking and listening, representing others and being represented by them, learn not just who these others are, but who they themselves may be, not just what others may mean but what they themselves may mean among others" (792). For the first two parts of the novel, the characters, and especially the nameless narrator, are not engaging conversation but disrupting it. In the last two parts, the narrator's conversations with others help clarify his relationships, but it is his conversation with himself, his concomitant responses to the questions of others and the questions he has posed to himself that engage the discourse field in a significant way. This engagement helps him define his identity and fix his place in the world.

The conversation of the characters is available to both

implied audiences. Members of a Native audience might be more concerned with the content of the conversation, matching it to their own experiences, but what is most important to them is that the conversation does create place and identity, thus nurturing survival. Members of a non-Native audience might puzzle over the disrupted stories but also cheer the victory of one individual over his personal demons. Both implied readers, whether Native or non-Native, can be represented by and projected into a value-building discourse created by the cultural voices defining themselves and others.

However, there is another level of conversation *about* the characters that the text engages, one designed to confront a Native reader. In many ways, the text addresses the difficulties of contemporary Native American existence. The death of family members, racism, unemployment, cultural confusion, disrupted family structures, and the loss of some aspects of traditional lifestyles and religion would all be familiar themes to Native readers. An individual troubled by the paradoxes of contemporary experience is at the center of meaning in *Winter in the Blood*. Welch has noted the foregrounding of these problems when he says "I have chosen to write about two guys [in *Winter in the Blood* and *The Death of Jim Loney*] who sort of have self-limiting worlds, who don't try very hard to rise above what they are, because they interest me. I've seen people like this all my life. . . . They are more tortured people" (qtd. in Bevis 169). Welch acknowledges that he must meet the expectation of what he considers to be a "large audience" of Indians and "paint pictures of reservation life as it really is" (qtd. in McFarland 8). The cultural conversation about the problems of contemporary experience implies a Native reader who will appreciate the novel's verisimilitude. Welch continues, "I would hate to have the people who are the most important people tell me that I'm doing it wrong" (8).[3] Indeed the Native reader's involvement and response is vital to Welch's ability to generate texts because it assures that his voice is heard as part of a broad discourse field. He explains, "It gives me a vote of confidence and helps to authenticate the kind of things I'm doing" ("Conversation" 108). As the narrator reestablishes conversation and narration in the novel to move toward some individual definition and continuance, so does the novel position itself in a larger conversation aimed at redefining identity and promoting survival.

These goals rise out of the dual conversations in the mediation of the novel's text. To more completely embed the text in the Native discourse field, Welch adopts the highly ironic and self-reflexive mode of Indian humor.[4] Obviously, the humor in the novel is intended to satisfy both implied readers; perhaps, however, it satisfies them in different ways. A non-Native audience can easily identify the role of humor in alleviating the somber tone of much of the book, while the implied Native reader can see a comment on contemporary Native problems. Welch also uses the humorous portrayals to undermine stereotypical responses, by showing the common humanity under the stereotype. As Kate Vangen writes, "Often Welch . . . confronts expectations by first obliging them, then subverting them. Of all the negative and racist things that might be said about Indians, Welch has Indians say (or do) them first" (197).

Welch himself defines Indian humor as "a humor based on presenting people in such a way that you're not exactly making fun of them, but you're seeing them for what they are and then you can tease them a little bit. That's a lot of Indian humor—teasing, and some plays on words; Indians are very good at puns" (qtd. in Coltelli 192). The puns are numerous in the novel, and both audiences respond to them. There is also a teasing of the characters by the author, which neatly meshes with an existing Native discourse field of sociopolitical dimensions. The implied Native reader can respond to the Indian humor in many of the scenes. Because this cultural conversation about characters emerges from a non-disrupted field of Indian humor, the disrupted discourse is given a context and the Native reader is anchored in one secure perspective. Deloria ties humor to the center of a conversation on contemporary problems: "The more desperate the problem, the more humor is directed to describe it" (147). This perspective then encourages a fusion in the implied Native reader of historical and political commentary through the ironic humor of an alienated individual trying not to become involved.

Most of the characters are presented in such a way that they are not overtly humiliated but rather in a way that reveals their true qualities and opens them up for teasing. The old lady is a speechless presence, but her thoughts are of killing the Cree girl because the Cree are traditional enemies, though no wars have been fought since the nineteenth century. The girl on the other hand imagines herself as Raquel Welch. Teresa's opinions about Indian men and Lame Bull's notions about being a rancher also set them up for teasing. All are teased by the author/narrator about attitudes that are identifiable in contemporary Native American communities and conversations and that make up the backbone of everyday dialogue.

Once the narrative moves to the point of describing life in the towns, the teasing takes on a bizarre appearance. People like the airplane man, the barmaid from Malta, and the two suits become merely names that describe some aspect of their lives. The teasing soon centers on the almost surrealistic, disconnected barroom conversations that both implied readers can find humorous. The narrator even self-reflexively teases himself as he tells of walking the streets with a purple teddy bear and boxes of candy or, at the end, of offering Agnes a creme de menthe instead of a wedding ring. The teasing is given a mythological resonance when the narrator's revelation about his lineage is tied to the horse's fart, since such scatological humor abounds in the ancient stories. Moreover, the dead man in oatmeal, the stuck coffin, and drunken flies occupy some self-consciously paradoxical ground between slapstick and metaphor. While Indian humor, as Welch defines it, provides a foundation for Native discourse, he quickly expands and directs it toward his own mediational goals. For the Native reader, the humor confirms survival; as Deloria writes, "In humor life is redefined and accepted" (146).

The stabilizing discourse of Indian humor carries both implied readers to the final two parts of the novel. There, the discourse of the characters, especially of the narrator, becomes more coherent and complete. The conversations *of* and *about* characters merge. After the death of the old woman, Teresa's demeanor becomes more serious and Lame Bull becomes more considerate, or perhaps the narrator is just now realizing the true human emotion behind their words as he begins to close the distance between himself and the world around him. As the stories of the grandmother and of Mose are completed in one day, the narrator now wants all stories to come out right, and he tries to create narratives that sustain and explain. He tells the Horns that Agnes is inside the house. He even creates a complete story for Bird, which allows him to turn guilt into grief. More importantly, Yellow Calf and the narrator communicate on a deeply personal and significant level, as Yellow Calf, with his story about the old woman, ties him into tribal and personal oral tradition. This continuum establishes an identity and place for the narrator. Yellow Calf's final silence when asked the implied question about fathering Teresa, is overcome by the previously outlined discourse context of the characters. Silence speaks eloquently. The revelation is a catalyst for reconnections to family, the land, the animals around him, and to his own memories of the past that have paralyzed him. In his struggle to save the wild-eyed cow, he remarks, "I crouched and spent the next few minutes planning my new life" (169).

The revelation of his grandfather's identity completes the narrative about his grandmother's life, and the story of Teresa's birth clarifies the narrator's tie to the drifter Doagie, explaining why First Raise took him to see Yellow Calf. This burst of illumination provides one coherent narrative thread and shows him that distance and relationship are not antithetical, that consistency in connection is possible over time and space. First Raise's hunting story kept him going for a long time; perhaps this story will keep the narrator going too.

The narrator's changed perceptions about himself, the people around him, and the natural world generate the author's final position about the narrator's role in the cultural conversation. Identity is reconstituted by a transforming of distance from family, from land, from oral tradition, from traditional experience, from guilt and from pain, into a new standpoint where distance can have a positive psychic value. If he can survive, others can. While such connections may always be tentative and in need of regeneration, they do provide a survival path for contemporary Indian people. Only by facing real problems can real answers be found. The world of stalking white men is revealed to be as much a result of the narrator's individual dis-ease as it is of the cockeyed world of social and historical displacement. Welch does not encourage scapegoating while he describes reality. The cockeyed nature of the world requires a change of perception more than it does violence or nostalgia. The Native reader is encouraged to probe a psychological explanation for contemporary problems that might exist separate from a historical one. Such an approach may not be traditional in Blackfeet or Gros Ventre culture, but it may help combat the bad medicine, and if it does, it promotes cultural survival and identity. As the novel moves both readers toward an understanding of connectedness, a more Native world view is reinforced and a traditional perspective, which can combat social malaise and marginalization, is suggested. If the world is cockeyed, an individual's balance may help right it.

While both implied readers will respond to the disrupted narratives in the conversation of the characters and to some of the humor, certain discourse fields are alluded to and engaged, allowing the non-Native implied reader easier access. The confused drunken barroom conversations provide common ground for both readers, but discourse concerning *Field & Stream*, 1950s Westerns, and detective stories helps create a context that locates the non-Native reader on familiar cultural ground. Robert Gish discusses how the text makes mocking use of the characteristics of the mystery or detective novel and the novel of intrigue. Mysteries abound, such as Mose and First Raise's death and Teresa's birth, while the search for Agnes provides the framework for a mock intrigue. Gish concludes that the ironic use of such elements "provides a way of synthesizing views which see the novel as either tragic or comic; either a native American or a non-ethnic book; either a modern psychological novel or a Western, either regional or universal; either one thing or the other" (45). Owens notes how the Fisher King, a figure in grail romance and Eliot's *The Wasteland*, is humorously used. More specifically, he links the novel to Bellow's *Henderson the Rain King* (*Other* 132–34). William Bevis identifies an Indian plot in contemporary Native American novels, which he opposes to the standard white plot, concluding, "In *Winter in the Blood*, the white existential plot, the Indian homing plot, and the first-person poetic brilliance coincide" ("Native" 610). Clearly the discourse field of contemporary literature, both popular and highbrow is being engaged. Employing such discourse and combining it with a variety of other discourse fields allow Welch effectively to address his mediation to both implied audiences.

The non-Native implied reader readily sees the familiar contours of the narrator's detachment from his own experience and disaffiliation with the institutions of contemporary life. As a story about alienation and psychological trauma, the novel's text neatly fits into contemporary American literary discourse. The modern American protagonist typically searches for connection and meaning. As Ihab Hassan concludes, "Alienation of the self from society used to be, and in a sense remains, the basic assumption of the modern novel"

(104). Welch's nameless narrator fits neatly within that audience expectation, though for a purpose, as I will discuss later, that differs from most contemporary writers. While an implied non-Native reader might not know if Welch succeeded in painting "pictures of reservation life as it really is," that reader would recognize the familiar contemporary stereotype of the aimless, drunken young Indian. As Welch explores his narrator's psychological composition and his family's troubled relationships, he gives a human face to his narrator. Because his problems and emotions are universal, the implied non-Native reader must look beyond the stereotype. Given the massive ignorance about Native Americans and their consistent cartoonization even today, it is not surprising that Native American writers often feel that the first step they must take with non-Native readers is that of stereotype negating. But Welch's goals extend beyond this step.

Verisimilitude in the account of reservation life is important if the non-Native reader is to understand reservation social problems and act effectively in the future. Welch acknowledges that his work should build the social conscience of the implied non-Native reader. He comments, "I hope my writing can keep reminding people that there is an Indian situation, problem, or however you want to put it—and that it's still going on. They should be reminded of it by the writer, by the artist" ("Conversation" 110). Welch introduces a discourse about Native characters with which the non-Native reader is unfamiliar, but he does so by engaging many familiar threads and evoking the fabric if not the pattern. He does so because he believes that literature can contribute to cross-cultural understanding. He concludes:

> Well, I think it can be very simple if other cultures want to just take the time to read about another culture. I think most Indian writers would probably think that they are telling about a way of life, either traditional or contemporary, that Indians have lead or are leading and this in essence is the truth of it. And so

it's not a matter of Indian people, Indian writers, getting out whatever message they feel is necessary; it's a question of people receiving that message. (qtd. in Coltelli 196)

As the non-Native audience follows the shift from the conversation of characters to the conversation about characters, it is guided toward a redirection of the epistemological underpinning of the non-Native discourse fields. As the narrator begins to reveal a changed perception of himself, his past, his family, and the world around him, the implied non-Native reader is escorted to a question—why has this come about? The key to answering that question lies in a necessary shift of precognitive assumptions. As Bakhtin suggests, a translation of the language of the other can generate a different reality, and Welch believes that the shift can be accomplished:

> When you are immersed in the Indian culture, notions of reality just necessarily change because there is this tradition, which isn't far in the past. So I don't think it has had a chance to be extinguished entirely from the Blackfeet culture or any other northern plains cultures, which are the ones I know. So, I think young people do have a notion of what their traditional forebears [sic] believed and how they saw life, how they saw their spiritual existence; and so, if you can see that and somehow translate it into contemporary experience I think you are being a part of that notion of reality, which to today's rational thinkers, I suppose, would be considered a form of surrealism. (qtd. in Coltelli 188)

Welch's much discussed surrealism has complex sources, but for the nameless narrator of *Winter in the Blood*, his immersion in this notion of reality, however tentative or flawed, offers him hope. Non-Native readers must take some of that journey with him if they are to construct a meaningful answer to the mystery of the narrator's healing. Questions of repression, guilt, and alienation seem to predominate in the first half of the novel. However, after the description of the narrator's dream, the surrealistic quality of the events in the novel becomes foregrounded. The non-Native implied reader may wonder whether the flashbacks and surreal events should be viewed as something more than just psychological disorientation. Allen points out that in the Native notion of reality "dream and vision are synonymous" (*Sacred* 91). Thus non-Native readers have to give up their familiar psychological understanding. Allen contends that the use of flashbacks and surrealistic methods to solve problems posed by the different white and Indian understandings of the relationship between time and event makes Indian experience and world view comprehensible to white readers (*Sacred* 151–52).[5] Or, as Welch admits, "I like to warp reality a little bit" (qtd. in Lincoln, *Native* 150). As has been noted, the warping allows an opening for Indian humor to highlight the conversation about characters, but more importantly it encourages the implied non-Native reader to ponder the meaning of events in new ways.

One motif, which both audiences will identify and share, is the appreciation and expectation of the act of revelation. Revelations of a hero's hidden repressed memories and of his obscured heritage are nothing new to Western literature. But a layering of Native world view and epistemology creates resonance for the non-Native reader, a resonance that guides him or her to inquire whether the revelations have wider meaning to the narrator and to the author than regaining ancestral roots. Owens and especially Allen have followed William Thackeray in describing the vision quest nature of the novel's process of revelation.[6] Welch, however, has specifically denied such a dimension unless it is referred to as an "abstract vision quest" (qtd. in Coltelli 187). Thackeray sees a more literal ritualization of the action; the narrator's despondent, drunken wanderings result in a ritual purification similar to what occurs in Gros Ventre ritual.[7] The most convincing points of his discussion are where he identifies events in the text such as the dream, the bath, and the educational discussions with the grandfather. But, of course, these elements could be established through a reference to Propp's analysis of folktales as well as a discussion of Crazy Lodge initiation. My point is that these very elements are the ones to which both a Native and non-Native audience would respond. The common expectations of revelation are on an "abstract" level. The implied Native readers would most likely recognize the value of dreams and visions, sweat lodge-related activities, and the wisdom of elders, especially relatives. The implied non-Natives might expect the revelation of his true heritage to produce meaning. Yet, the Native paradigm would resonate enough to keep the non-Native reader from closure, because he or she would also sense the essentially mythic pattern of meaning here. Even in the question of revelation, enough of the Native notion of reality would disturb the non-Native's expected construction of meaning, misreading leading to rereading and reconsideration.

Moreover, the question of the narrator's "distance" decenters both the reinforcing of Native world view, thus encouraging reevaluation, and the guiding of the implied non-Native reader into that very perspective. Much has been written on the idea of distance, both on the narrator's emotional, physical, and spiritual distance, which creates the "winter" in his blood, and on the sense of distance he senses in Yellow Calf and that he feels himself after he saves the cow.[8] The first sense of distance Welch and most of his critics agree constitutes the central emotional atmosphere of the first half of the novel. The other sense of distance Kunz refers to as an aesthetic one (97) and Jahner identifies as one that turns dreams into fact ("Quick" 44). Both of these concepts are useful in addressing how the second sense of distance might realign a Native audience's tendency to identify too closely with the vision of connectedness offered in the representation of Native world view. Yellow Calf's distance is difficult if not impossible to attain today since he is part of a different era. He is distant from the contemporary world yet connected to the natural world. Paradoxically, the narrator links the distance in his eyes with his connection to the animal and spirit worlds. The distance of connectedness, or what Welch calls "that other distance" (161), and not the nostalgia of trying to live the old ways, is a more realizable goal for a Native audience concerned with survival. However, there is still a distance felt by all the characters from complete identification with Yellow Calf's vision. As Welch says, "I've always balanced that contrast between the sense of modern desolation and desperation and the old ways" (qtd. in Bruchac 316). Even for the Native reader, distance cannot be done away with, it can only be used to create a balance. The distance the narrator feels in the cold rain is punctuated by direct references to the reader as "you." This sudden turning on both readers is important for Stephen Tatum's vision of the paradoxical sense of distance that constitutes "the novel's impossible project of simultaneously eliminating and preserving 'distance'" (76).[9] The challenge to the non-Native reader is the paradoxical one of feeling a distance in the rain and feeling connected and alive. Such a standpoint presupposes that the implied readers have been brought to a perspective where they can appreciate and create meaning in a personal, aesthetic, or even perhaps spiritual revelation of a connectedness to the world around them. Indeed, in the last parts of the novel, as the narrator's thawing begins, the non-Native reader is shifted into a perspective that acknowledges a more Native sense of connectedness and mythic signification. The paradoxical sense of distance then is necessary to ensure closure through a perspective other than one that searches for mere psychological unity.

This perspective rests on a Native sense of connectedness to place, ancestors, and animals. Welch suggests that this perspective is achieved during moments when "you realize that this isn't something apart from you. This is part of what we're all in—everything that is around us" (qtd. in Bevis, "Dialogue" 181). As the narrator is moved into a more Native sense of connectedness, so are both implied readers, but the non-Native reader must do this by creating meaning through connectedness. Clearly Yellow Calf's story connects the narrator to family, history, and tribal identity, but it also connects him to a community—a community of spirits and animals— where time and distance do not separate. The narrator says: "And so we shared this secret in the presence of ghosts, in wind that called forth the muttering tepees, the blowing snow, the white air of the horses' nostrils. The cottonwoods behind us, their dead white branches angling to the threatening clouds, sheltered these ghosts as they had sheltered the camp that winter. But there were others, so many others" (159). Charles Ballard has noted that this is a community not just of kinspeople but also of animals. He believes that the changed perspective of the narrator allows him a distance which, like Yellow Calf's, is equidistant in time and space, a necessary position for "balance that is achieved by being part of nature's scheme and also the center of one's world" (70).

In the last part of the novel and in the Epilogue, the narrator is able to talk to Mose and First Raise as if there were no distance between them. Previously he was unable even to look at their graves. When Yellow Calf asked him to say hello to First Raise, the narrator could make no sense of a request to address the dead. He now feels so close to them that he can speak to them with no thought of separation. The narrator also experiences the present in a way that fuses the past, present, and future, so they are not distanced from each other. He can move through all aspects of the connectedness because each event reveals multiple meanings. Allen refers to this perception of reality as the achronological, ritual time represented in the novel (*Sacred* 93–94).

The interconnectedness of Native world view is revealed as the narrator moves closer to a position like Yellow Calf's, who is so connected to animals that he can converse with them. As the book closes, the narrator, recognizing his own connection to animals, is remorseful for shooting the hawk (130) and for running the cows (139). He absolves Bird of guilt in Mose's death (144) just as he absolves himself and the wild-eyed cow by saving her. After the ordeal, he can almost hear the magpie talking to him (172).[10] The net effect is to allow the narrator, through connectedness, to inhabit a space, to become a part of "everything that is around us." In this world where ghosts are present and time distinctions blurred, dreams tell the truth, and animals talk, the implied non-Native reader is encouraged to translate the meaning of the narrator's change through a more Native epistemological structure, a structure necessary to right the cockeyed world.

As the narrator begins to perceive the world with a new perspective, his sense of identity is negotiated. Owens sees this process in terms of a renewal: "a recovery dependent upon a renewed sense of identity as Indian, as specifically Blackfoot . . ." (*Other* 131). Indeed this sense of continuity of Indian identity is bolstered by Welch when he writes, "Whites have to adopt an identity; Indians already have one" (qtd. in Craig 184). This sense of identity gets communal expression when the narrator develops a renewed respect for his elders, perhaps even adopting the position of helper or apprentice to old Yellow Calf. Possibly he now understands how bad medicine works and can struggle to rid himself and his family of it. He seems to see renewed value in his immediate family. His attitude toward the Horns, the girl in the car, his would-be wife, Lame Bull, and Teresa demonstrate some improved sense of respect and hospitality. As Yellow Calf was the hunter for his grandmother, so he is the hunter of a wife. He participates in traditional customs when he throws the tobacco into the grave. He even understands why his family lives on that particular farm, and he regains for the family its identity. These elements compose his communal and cultural sense of self.

Concurrently, his mythic sense of identity evolves from his grandparents and their association with the characters of Blackfeet mythology. Owens associates the repeated use of the names "Old Man" and "Old Woman," referring to the narrator's grandparents, with the first man and first woman of Blackfeet origin stories; this is "an appropriate association since it is from this pair that the narrator inherits identity and authenticity" (*Other* 143). His mythic identity establishes him as a grandchild of the mythic creators. As he seeks to piece together his world, to transforms parts of it, he mirrors the actions of Napi, or Old Man, even talking to the animals as Napi did. Indeed some of the tricksteresque episodes in which the narrator becomes involved, echo the wandering, comic travels of Napi. Both Napi and the narrator seem to have trouble with women and with remembering what their purpose is. As he rises from the mud while rescuing the cow, the narrator is reborn, planning his "new life." In that mud, with the "smell of dead things," also lie Mose and First Raise from whom he no longer feels separated. He talks with Bird and Bird replies. The emergence from the mud is reminiscent of Napi's creation of mankind out of clay.[11] Note that Welch has chosen a symbolic action that could also echo the Christian creation story where God makes man out of dust, thus conferring in two systems mythic status to the event.

On a sociological level, he has been a drunk who has let distance define his relations to others and himself. But he has rejected the role of barfly, Indian drunk. He has even chosen not to become an outlaw. At first socially passive, he moves toward a more active stance. The narrator seems to have denied Indian society but now he understands more of its "thinking" and how this thinking defines identity and opens up a role to play that transforms distance into balance. He is in a position to accept contemporary Indian society, whatever its limitations and imperfections. He will not let society marginalize him anymore. By the end of the novel, it appears he is becoming a better son, more understanding and appreciative. Perhaps he might go on to make a good husband and a good stepson. His emerging understanding of animals might even suggest he could become an accomplished rancher.

Of the four narratives of identity, Welch foregrounds the

psychological story of the young man coming to grips with the guilt he feels at the death of his brother and his father. His repressed memories of the past surface and allow him to absolve himself of the blame. The guilt and negation that have dominated his life have also arrested his development, his achievement of a unified sense of self. As distance turns into balance, he accepts death as a part of a larger whole and thus matures as an individual.

Perhaps the narrator is now ready to call himself by a name. He has developed a sense of identity on a number of planes. But the most telling mark of this new maturity might be that he is finally in a position to tell his narrative of multiple identity. As Owens concludes, "In the tradition of Native American storytelling, the narrator has asserted some kind of order and significance within his own life by telling the narrative we have just read" (*Other* 144). The cockeyed world may still be there, but Welch creates a mediational narrative strategy that can give both implied readers a means to put it back in balance.

No Boundaries, Only Transitions

Ceremony

◆

Ceremony has received wide praise from almost the first day of publication. Presently it is still the mainstay of many courses in Native American literature. It is increasingly read in Contemporary American literature classes. The novel remains popular among Native students and among sophisticated critics of contemporary literature. The wide cross-cultural attention is testimony to the novel's richly textured and mediational character; Silko's various audiences are challenged, satisfied, and challenged again.

Silko's novel circles around critical, personal, and cultural decisions about what to fuse from the old and the new. However, the novel expresses these decisions in terms of the various discourse fields it engages and then modifies. Silko's oral influences emphasize the way her utterance will define identity and mesh with other discourse: "One of the things I was taught to do from the time I was a little child was to listen to the story about you personally right now. To take all of that in for what it means right now, and for what it means for the future. But at the same time to appreciate how it fits in with what you did yesterday, last week, maybe ironically, you know drastically different" (qtd. in Coltelli 141). With a similar dialogic orientation, implied readers are alerted at the very start of the novel to the fact that everything they will read is actually Thought Woman's narrative. She contends that the evolving stories in the novel are the only defense against evil. The stories alone will replenish the life of the people. As in the narratives Silko heard while growing up, the stories in the novel will define and continue life, allowing readers to appreciate "the idea that one story is only the beginning of many stories, and the sense that stories never truly end" ("Language" 56).

Throughout the novel, Silko's goals are truly mediational as she seeks to translate the languages of the Other, but for both Native and non-Native fields of discourse, she must answer what has been asked before, acknowledge previous discourse, and advance cultural conversations. Yet she must also open up a field of access where Native implied readers can mediate their experiences just as the non-Native implied reader must. Ultimately, the text leads the reader to validate Native epistemology—a central goal in the mediation of contemporary Native American literature—and to appreciate the new structures of meaning that mediation creates.

Clearly, Silko's discourse fields come from arenas as widely separate as ancient stories of the Pueblo peoples, which we tend to call "myths," and World War II soldiers-on-leave stories that come from mainstream culture. Mary Slowik notes the adventure and detective story elements in Silko's novel. Dasenbrock identifies the novel as having "generic affiliations with this naturalistic tradition of American literature" in its use of the themes of the postwar novel (315). Ruoff writes about how Silko's work incorporates Keres traditional narratives and Robert Nelson ties the novel to an ongoing discourse about Laguna place and landscape, exploring how the stories grow out of the land.[1] He reveals how the intersection of myth and place anchor Tayo's story into the webwork of all other kiva stories. Silko observes, "The structure of Pueblo expression resembles something like a spider's web—

with many threads radiating from a center, criss-crossing each other. . . . Words are always with other words, and the other words are almost always in a story of some sort" ("Language" 54–55).

But since her text draws from even larger fields of contemporary American discourse and traditional Laguna and Navajo discourse, the critical decisions center on how to embed her artistic choices in the continuing multi-cultural conversations. Her new textual structure must be a new ceremony, one growing and evolving, a contribution to Laguna ceremonial discourse, and an enactment of the goals of the novel itself. Allen notes: "Two of *Ceremony's* major themes are the centrality of environmental integrity and the pacifism that is its necessary partner, common motifs in American literature in the last quarter of the twentieth century. Silko develops them entirely out of a Laguna/Keres perspective, for both themes are fundamental to the fabric of Keres pueblo life and thought" (*Sacred* 96). Allen perceives these discourses as played out through the introduction of the ideas and values "of ecology, antiracist, and antinuclear movements," which advance the plot and major themes in the novel (*Sacred* 145). These contemporary discourses contribute to the cultural conversation on modern American life, but Silko engages them not just to have her say, but to redirect the way they articulate these values. Her method is subversive in the best sense. Per Seyersted misunderstands the introduction of this level of the text when he complains, "Occasionally there are passages or scenes which seem contrived, and in certain descriptions of what the whites have done, Silko's expression comes closer to that of the activist than we would expect" (34). Actually most non-Native readers expect a great deal more activist discourse from any Native American writer. Silko gives just enough to establish a historical and sociological perspective, then uses that basis to alter Western epistemology.

The experienced reader of Western fiction can readily identify in *Ceremony* the outlines of a protest novel. As a result of his participation in the American army in World War II, the main character appears to be the victim of social forces. His people have been oppressed by an indifferent and often hostile dominant culture. They have been beaten, robbed, and victimized. His traditional beliefs are under seige by an intolerant world view. Silko even brings in the atomic bomb as the ultimate act of cultural and global violation. Obviously, in this discourse context, books and stories about World War II, minority rights, poverty, and prejudice create a field upon which *Ceremony* builds, answers, and extends. Reference to this field encourages implied readers to exercise their liberal conscience. They search for a sociological analysis of events in the text and come up with insights that Silko encourages. For instance, she describes the white doctors' attitudes toward Tayo's communal orientation. They want him to think only of himself and to stop using words like "we" and "us" (125). Similarly, when Tayo cuts the wire on the mountain, he cuts away the social lie of brown-skinned inferiority.

However, while these passages fit neatly into a tradition of social analysis in Western literature, they are not so familiar to implied Native readers. Silko's use of social analysis may lead for them to new insight into how this lie, embedded in American discriminatory discourse, has become internalized. While the use of Western discourse might also respond to previous Western discourse, Silko's goal is mediational since Tayo cuts through that social lie so that he can get to a deeper truth about a mythic relationship between whites and Indians.

An excellent example of how mediation shifts perception and discourse can be seen when the text shifts toward the middle of the novel. After a long, relatively straightforward discussion of displaced people like Helen Jean and Gallup, and subjects like Indian drinking and war veterans, Tayo tries to vomit out everything, "all the past, all his life" (168). After this purging, the text shifts to a Native perspective on the sociological narrative, developing an Indian parable about the land and spiritual destruction. Then, Tayo voices his belief in the necessity of transitions, and Silko gives us the story of how Sun, with the help of Spiderwoman, beats the evil Gambler and releases the rain clouds. These Native and mythic perspectives on the events described balance and challenge the previous sociological perspective. Both implied readers become primarily involved with maneuvering through the transitions in the text. However, the mechanism of mediation here also works to validate each perspective, revealing their strengths and limitations. Both implied readers are led to question which perspective is more complete, which explains more, and which leads to healing and unity. The dialogism of the text leads implied readers to seek ways to merge and understand both perspectives.[2] At this point in the novel, Silko does not provide any clear path to produce this healing. Tayo and the implied readers must make their own transitions. Such action prepares them for the time later in the novel when the transitions are supplied.

Iser sees this process of the creation and reevaluation of meaning not as a jumble of dizzying switches between perspectives, but as the very essence of a dynamic process of self-correction that is reading itself. He concludes: "In the literary text, not only is the background unformulated and variable, but its significance will also change in accordance with the new perspectives brought about by the foregrounded elements; the familiar facilitates our comprehension of the unfamiliar, but the unfamiliar in turn restructures our comprehension of the familiar" (94). To satisfy the discourse expectations of both audiences, Silko must restructure how each audience values truth, reality, and knowledge. The result is not just an increased appreciation of Native world view by non-Native audiences, but an evolution of Native world view through the "constant interaction between meanings" that Holquist characterizes as Bakhtinian dialogism.[3]

Just as the social discourse is transformed into myth, so

must be the psychological discourse. The novel begins with a Laguna discourse frame and then swiftly moves to a fragmented narrative that mirrors Tayo's mental state. As the text progresses, the narrative structure becomes more linear, though not necessarily more chronological. When Tayo is healed, the text becomes more coherent, until by the end it does not foreground fragmentation. This pattern of healing and growth, familiar from Western psychological novels, is translated into Laguna mythic terms: as Tayo heals and the fragmentation of his life and of the text retreat, he emerges fully into the world of myth and ceremony, seeing the web of stories.

In discussing what originally caused Tayo's illness, Allen argues that Tayo's illness stems from his acceptance of the witchery's mistaken perception that humans and other creatures are not part of a larger oneness: "The cure for that misunderstanding, for Tayo, was a reorientation of perception so that he could know directly that the true nature of being is magical and that the proper duty of the creatures, the land, and human beings is to live in harmony with what is" (*Sacred* 125). Betonie informs Tayo that his sickness is part of something larger than himself and his cure would be found "in something great and inclusive of everything" (125). Tayo's ultimate realization is that he has never been crazy, that he was simply always perceiving the timeless way things truly are, without the artificial boundaries imposed by Western thought, especially psychology (192, 246). Past and present, and all levels of identity, are one.

Indeed, the whole question of identity, which is at the heart of psychological discourse, is mediated in *Ceremony*. At the start, Tayo feels bereft of identity, and non-Native readers tend to follow the information presented about his mother, his upbringing, and the death of his brother to try to piece together a conventional image of self; however, he comes to realize that his identity is bound up with Laguna's identity, with something larger than his own psyche. It is this insight that leads him to the revelation of who he is, and not an acceptance of repressed unconscious material—which psychoanalytic theory would have us believe is the path to integration and identity.[4]

As we swift our discussion from the goals of mediation to the form of mediation in *Ceremony*, we could explore how changes in typeface and text formats in the novel indicate shifts to new fields of utterance and new context. A study of the spacial breaks as opposed to chapter breaks might reveal how Silko expresses the flow of one unified field of mediational experience existing in the novel. This field is designed to thwart linear chronological development by allowing events, since they are not locked into chapters, to resonate and return later in the text. The end result is to dismantle Western notions of narrative structure and time so as to allow Native and mediative perception to create meaning.

Much of Silko's method can be revealed by an analysis of the juxtaposition of poetry and prose in the text. The lines in the text that look like poetry indicate a self-reflexive and consciously Western form, yet they serve to carry across the traditional communal and mythic discourse of Laguna.[5] These lines, which are referred to as Thought Woman's cognition taking the shape of reality, establish a Native discourse context linked to past conversations as well as an interpretative frame. It is this frame that will ultimately shift the implied reader's perception to create an experience that achieves one of Silko's major goals. Ideally Silko would like both implied readers to hear the poetry lines, for she feels they are the closer to oral discourse contexts.[6] In contrast to the poetic sections of the text, the familiar Western sociological and psychological account of a shattered war veteran is presented in prose, disjointed and disrupted from its expected discourse context. The prose presents a reality, but a contorted reality. Initially the oral, mythic text is the most coherent, though its context is unfamiliar to non-Native readers, while the fragmented psychological narrative has context but no coherence. Dreams, a traditional Native source for meaning, are scrambled. The Native audience must search for the context of the psychological narrative. Tayo, who does not appear in the poetry at the beginning of the book, feels in the prose sections as if he has no name, a verbal sign that could tie him equally to either the Native or the non-Native discourse spheres.

The poetry is at first thematically separate from the prose, just as Tayo's past is cut off from his present. For the non-Native implied reader, the familiar war story discourse is cut off from the exotic discourse in the poetry, a discourse that expresses another level of the life and experience of Laguna Pueblo. An ideological and epistemological translation must take place to create meaning from the various discourse elements in the poetry and prose sections. Both audiences must begin a mediational process to appreciate a new discourse field, to change their sense of what is real and what is meaningful.

As the novel continues, the text teases both audiences by pretending to slip smoothly into the familiar Western discourse about returned veterans or even returned native sons; however, in the middle of the novel, the Laguna war stories are suddenly expressed in poetry rather than prose. As the reality-based stories are raised to myth, Silko emphasizes how myths grow, complement, and structure reality—how mythic discourse and practical discourse are built out of the same components.[7] In doing this, Silko contends that she is "trying to affect the old, old, old way of looking at the world" ("Conversation" 32).

Progressively, the form of Silko's text reveals one further goal—the merging of those categories Western discourse has termed myth and reality. The myth or poetry sections pace the progress of the prose (the section of the text that we read as describing reality). As Eliade reminds us, myth is always exemplary, providing "paradigms for all significant human acts" (*Myth and Reality* 18). The Laguna paradigms lead the reader to new events, and comment on action, but always lend a sense of order to the fragmented prose just as myth often does to reality. For example, the story of Sun who defeats the Gambler and releases the rain clouds (170) is a precursor of the myth in which hummingbird, fly, and buzzard purify the town. This purification story also foreshadows the return of the "clouds with round heavy bellies" (255) at the end of the novel, though now they are in the prose section. What is important here is not so much that poetic sections parallel prose sections, but that they are different expressions of the same phenomena.

One could further say that the poetic sections create meaning in the prose or more precisely that the interfacing between the two creates meaning for the implied readers as they initiate the ideological translation of the language of the Other. Facilitating this process is Silko's method of creating mediation. Silko, of course, never separates the two perceptual fields; instead, in the novel, she refers to them both as "story." Ts'eh reminds Tayo that the whites have stories about them as much as do the Indians—one person's story of reality is as real as the next person's. What is important is whether the stories end correctly and whether they create identity while holding off illness and death (232). Tayo must end the story in the terms of mediative mythic discourse and not in the sociological discourse of maladjusted war veterans and psychotic murders.

To do this both Tayo and the readers must employ a mythic way of knowing. They must be able to appreciate, in addition to other modes of knowing, this manner of giving meaning to events. Elaine Jahner reasons: "Through the narrative events of the novel, protagonist and reader gradually learn to relate myth to immediate action, cause to effect; and both reader and protagonist learn more about the power of story itself. The reader seeks to learn not only what happens to Tayo but how and why it happens. The whole pattern of cause and effect is different from most novels written from a perspective outside the mythic mode of knowledge" ("Act" 44). The prose becomes increasingly more coherent as both readers develop greater context for both spheres of discourse and various modes of perception. Though the chronology continues to move between past and present, the shifts are less jarring. Those distinctions that could be made between psychological, mythic, sociological, and communal narratives are conflated as all levels of narrative become one story. Tayo's personal story is presented first in the lines of poetry that follow the description of Betonie's ceremony (153) and then later in poetic form when the old men of the Pueblo recognize his role in the mythic level of reality (257). They acknowledge him as part of the ongoing life of the community; the discourse of the Pueblo has been elaborated to include him. Tayo's story has been tied in to the many stories that comprise Laguna discourse. Silko comments on the nature of such discourse when she describes old Ku'oosh's highly self-reflexive language, a discourse intricately tied with discussions of its own origin and all that has been said before. Each word is fragile, each has a story (34). Indeed, she contends, "language *is* story" (Language 56).

The text of *Ceremony* generates its own highly contextualized discourse in order to help non-Native implied readers see the relevancy of this discourse to Native world view and to help them ideologically translate and mediate their perceptions. The Native implied readers learn how to incorporate Western sociological and psychological discourse into their unified and *growing* world view. Betonie serves as a model here since he is able to translate Western and Native discourse spheres into new ceremonies and ceremonial visions. His phone books, newspapers, bear stories, and medicine pouches objectify mediation and cross-cultural discourse. Situated as he is physically between Native and non-Native, town and mountain, Betonie is, of course, the ideal person to effect the cure of Tayo and to help him mediate the discourses.

By the end of the novel, when Tayo has realized that there are no boundaries either in space or time, *Ceremony*'s form reflects this illumination. Tayo and the reader have begun to live the myth and, as Eliade concludes, "by 'living' the myths one emerges from profane, chonological time and enters a time that is of a different quality, a 'Sacred' Time at once primordial and indefinitely recoverable" (*Myth and Reality* 18). Tayo's dreams and his reality are acknowledged to be the same (222). As clouds gather, the spirits of the dead are present in much the same way that the dead return with the rain clouds as katchinas. The transition is complete when Josiah and Rocky wrap Tayo up and take him home—he is at last dreaming with his eyes open. Myth and reality have merged in the story still being told, the mediative discourse developing in both spheres. We must remember that the mythic story of the Destroyers is not a traditional Laguna narrative, but a translation, a mediation that both addresses and furthers Native discourse. And the external and illusory distinctions between prose and poetry are forced to reveal an underlying larger epistemological unity—a unity that mirrors Laguna epistemology but also enlarges it by enabling an appreciation of how the cross-cultural discourse context has generated new ceremonies, new mythic discourse. The oral tradition that nurtured Laguna narrative has been enriched and complemented.

In the final sections of the novel, the reading of the text turns into a dynamic interaction with the extra-textual world. Tayo's view of himself has become highly self-reflexive, but so has the reader's. Jahner concludes that the text brings readers face to face with their own way of understanding: "The ebb and flow of narrative rhythm in the novel creates an event in the process of telling about event. The entire process is ceremonial, and one learns how to experience it ceremonially by achieving various kinds of knowledge attained not through logical analysis but through narrative processes that have their own epistemological basis" ("Act" 39). The self-reflexive ability to perceive an event as the process of telling about event guides the reader into a ceremonial epistemology. As readers read and misread the nature of Tayo's sickness and the significance of events like the vision of Josiah during the War, they initiate a dynamic interaction with the text. They participate in creating meaning and change their perspective on the events in the text. However, their changing expectations and experiences are outside the text. Iser believes that it is this kind of communication that makes literary texts successful:

> The text must therefore *bring about* a standpoint from which the reader will be able to view things that would never have come into focus as long as his own habitual dispositions were determining his orientation, and what is more, this standpoint must be able to accommodate all kinds of different readers. . . . Thus the standpoint and the convergence of textual perspectives are closely interrelated, although neither of them is actually represented in the text, let alone set out in words. Rather they emerge during the reading process, in the course of which the reader's role is to occupy shifting vantage points that are geared to a prestructured activity and to fit the diverse perspectives into a gradually evolving pattern. (35)

Readers then grasp the different starting points of textual perspectives and their ultimate coalescence as the readers are moved through an evolving pattern to a concluding standpoint where meaning is both fixed and fluid. In the case of *Ceremony*, it is to a point where implied readers have an insight into how the Destroyers work in the world around them. They are given the perception to prepare them for future action and to initiate appropriate ceremonial responses.

The ceremonial process to which Jahner refers transforms the telling of the myth into the action of ritual. The act of reading becomes a ceremonial experience for both audiences because ceremonial language and event are performative. *Ceremony* draws on mythic narrative prototypes for its efficacy and authority. The mythic discourse of the novel prepares implied readers for the ceremony in which they will participate.[8]

To help us appreciate how the experience of reading the novel as a whole finally shifts the standpoint of both audiences out of the text and to a position where they both can create new meaning, I want to turn briefly to Todorov's analysis of ancient texts, which straddle oral and written traditions. He identifies two modes of speech that seem to structure such intermediary texts: *speech-as-action* and *speech-as-narrative*. It is clear that one of *Ceremony*'s goals is to shift the function of the written text from just incorporating various discourse contexts to evoking novel perceptual experiences where the reading of the novel becomes a new ceremony in itself. Todorov outlines these modes of discourse:

> First, in the case of speech-as-action, we react to the referential aspect of what is said [it is concerned with the act performed, which is not simply the utterance of the words.] . . . Speech-as-action is perceived as information, speech-as-narrative as a discourse. Second, and this seems contradictory, speech-as-narrative derives from the constantive mode of discourse, whereas speech-as-action is always performative. It is in the case of speech-as-action that the whole process of speaking assumes a primordial importance and becomes the essential factor of the message; speech-as-narrative deals with something else and evokes the presence of an action other than that of speech itself. (*Poetics* 59)

To create a written literature that will enhance the oral tradition, and provoke changes in the reader's epistemological structures, Silko must shift the mode of textual discourse. She must take speech-as-narrative, which underlines the contextual frame at the heart of Bakhtin's view of literature, and encourage the reader to perceive the way it ultimately functions as speech-as-action. As Thought Woman believes, the story comes into being when it is told. When readers are able to merge myth and reality, they are able to see the novel as a ceremony and as a prayer. And this is new meaning, information to both audiences. The act of utterance encoded in the text and emulated by the participant/reader takes on a "primordial importance" and becomes an "essential factor of the message" while the reading of the novel becomes a ceremony and a prayer.

On Mount Taylor, Tayo prays in the form of a song that the Dawn people sang. The novel begins, centers, and ends with the same word with which the song/prayer begins—*sunrise*. Consequently, the reading of the text becomes a prayer, becomes itself a new ceremony, yet this is a ceremony with roots in traditional religious discourse. Implied readers are placed in the position of Dawn priests. As Tayo's words and actions become completely integrated into a fused discourse, drawing upon sources as divergent as traditional Native ceremonies and the rhetoric of nuclear disarmament, the otherness of unfamiliar discourse spheres is overcome and at the same time revitalized. The text's effect shifts from speech-as-narrative to speech-as-action. Mediation is complete.

This analysis of one element of the form of the novel, the use of poetry and prose, has returned us to a discussion of the larger goals of the text. Certainly Silko leads all readers to an expanded appreciation of the multiple meaning of events and a new understanding of narrative. Indeed a new reality is created for implied readers as they find meaning in that which previously held only fictional meaning, hence no reality, no meaning. In *Ceremony*, myth becomes reality. Eliade identifies the ontological function of mythic epistemology when he writes "an object or act becomes real only insofar as it imitates or repeats an archetype. Thus, reality is acquired solely through repetition or participation; everything which lack an exemplary model is 'meaningless,' i.e., it lacks reality" (*Myth of the Eternal* 34). Tayo is in the middle of an epistemological struggle similar to that of many Native and non-Native readers as they attempt to endow the text with meaning. He may, however, be ahead of the game because deep down, he still believes in the old ways, that everything has a story and that mythic discourse *is* reality. As the novel moves to order his turmoil about what is real, it teaches its implied readers how to understand not only text, but also the events and forces in the world around us outside of the text. Humanity must unite to act against the work of the Destroyers.

However, to do this the reader must change, and most people are afraid of change. Tayo and Betonie know that those who are different often are scorned and become outcasts. Both audiences must acknowledge the growth of new myths and the renewal and evolution of the ceremonies. They must examine their attitudes toward different people, positions, and types of discourse. Their acts of mediation constitute Bakhtin's "ideological translation of the language of the other" and lead to a perspective on the text that merges the different spheres of discourse while continuing each of them. Readers must gain "the ear for the story and the eye for the pattern" (255), as Tayo did, before their perception can be transformed.

When readers reach this level of perception, a number of elements take on multiple significance. Silko would have both implied readers develop a "mind holding all thoughts together in a single moment" (237). The drought that has plagued Laguna can be seen as more than a phenomenon of the climate. It can be seen as the result of Laguna misbehavior and inattentiveness to the mythic/communal well-being (45). The people have followed the Destroyers who want them to think only of the loss and forget to renew and re-create the ceremonies (249). However, the drought is Tayo's drought as well. He is as barren of love as he is of identity. The drought is physical, communal, and mythic, and thus it must have a physical, communal, and mythic solution in the creation of a new ceremony. The rain clouds come to him and to Laguna when he has made his peace with the dead. The myths offer a path back to well-being not only for Tayo and Laguna, but also for the modern world which has not realized the extent of the drought of meaning in which it dwells. Implied readers must realize that the mixed-blood cattle can survive in the drought because they have the best qualities of both worlds. They can follow their instinct and become contemporary survivors. Readers must follow the cattle, Tayo, and Betonie and become epistemological mixed-blood survivors.

It is important for both Tayo and the implied readers to understand that there are no boundaries enclosing events into one-dimensional notions of reality. Tayo believes he has seen Josiah while looking at the Japanese, and the novel insists that we believe he has. Tayo talks with the hunter and Ts'eh in the mountains, and readers must know that they are indeed mythic beings with the same ability to be both human and animal that beings possessed in the age of myth. When Ts'eh folds her storm blanket, the snows stop.

These insights into the multiple significance of events help prepare the implied readers for the final fusion when Tayo sees the mountains around him and all the peoples of the world becoming part of Betonie's sand painting—the object that centers and orders the ceremony (246–47). Time boundaries, discourse boundaries, and racial boundaries all fall away. Everyone is included and harmonized in the struggle against the Destroyers who threaten the false sunrise of worldwide nuclear destruction. Defeating the Destroyers will require power from everywhere, even from the whites (150, 204). The novel's conclusion is set during the autumnal equinox when there is perfect order and balance between summer and winter, between night and day, as all the people of the world become one clan again.⁹

Tayo remarked earlier that Betonie's vision was a story he could feel happening. Reality, story, and myth are thus one, but one question remains. Ts'eh tells Tayo that the old men have been asking after him. They want to know who he is. Tayo's identity on all levels of meaning finally becomes clarified at the end of the novel when he establishes identity on each narrative level.

On the level of the psychological narrative, Tayo emerges from invisible, inarticulate white smoke to become a lover. His gutted emotions are healed by Ts'eh. He loves her, but he also loves all those important to him in his life. Tayo now knows that "nothing was ever lost as long as the love remained" (220). He is restored to his family almost as a son. Auntie now talks with him in the same way she talks to Robert and Grandma. He sees his own strength and knows he is healed. He has found power in the core of his being so that he can return to being a sane, balanced personality. He acknowledges his responsibility in a fragile world and demonstrates confidence in his ability to be whole and right. His psychological identity is solidly constituted.

In the end, Tayo's social identity centers around his position as a partial outsider, accepted now into the social structure but rejecting the imposed social definition of the drunk, shell-shocked veteran; as a result, his story does not have the ending of a tragic sociological narrative. He is a survivor just like the cattle are that he now cares for. No longer a scapegoat, he now feels responsible for those around him, a contributor to his Laguna society. Since he is a successful returned veteran, a warrior turned cattle man, the people now want to send to him veterans who are still troubled and other dysfunctional individuals for help in blending the two social worlds.

The communal narrative of identity concludes with Tayo assuming the role of a kiva priest. When he returns from the mountains, the old men come to inquire as to what he has to tell them. Perhaps they recognize that Tayo's trip into the mountains is the same trip that the elders make when they want to pray for rain. He now is an elder, a messenger, and a bringer of blessings since he has seen A'moo'ooh, carrier of life. The people will now be blessed, healed, purified. He crosses the river returning to the village like a katchina (182), or religious initiate. He is now a protector of Laguna, a caretaker of the rain plants. He can tell the people of the new ceremony and they will listen.

The mythic narrative creates an identity for Tayo by depicting his role as one who struggles against the Destroyers. He knows who he is in the myth as well as in the world around him. He knows what he must do; however, he also is a culture hero and as such, he functions like Arrowboy or Sun. Perhaps it is even more accurate to say that he acts like Hummingbird and Fly, who restored the people and the world. In Tayo's story, there is an echo of the old stories of orphans who bring new insights, and of Arrowboy (247). Wiget's analysis of the novel underscores the importance Tayo's identity as a culture hero: "A ceremony is required to reintegrate Tayo's self by reimpressing upon his fragmented psyche the whole mythic pattern of the culture hero and his quest, thus restoring the shape of his personal and communal history and reestablishing his identity" (*Native* 87).

As Wiget points out, it is important to see that all of these levels of identity support each other. Moreover, the identities are conflated in such a way that the mythic and psychological, and the social and communal, are all perceived by both audiences as unified. Silko's sense of character identity extends beyond simple metaphors of continuity and survival to the complex processes Clifford refers to as utilizing "appropriation, compromise, subversion, masking, invention, and revival" (338). On the mountain, these processes combine Betonie's vision and the reality of the cows; the she-elk and the woman, Ts'eh; the hunter and the mountain lion; the hunter whom Coyote bewitched in the myth/poetry passages and the bewitched Tayo in the prose. Mytic and psychological levels of identity must be invented and revived by Ts'eh and Tayo's love. The identity given by the ceremony must appropriate and subvert the social role of the drunken ex-veteran. Tayo's new communal identity as bringer of blessings to the community must combine with his personal love for Ts'eh, Josiah, and Rocky. And the mask must be uncovered as Tayo realizes what Grandma always knew: the stories are all the same; only the names change.

Mythic Verism

Bearheart: The Heirship Chronicles

◆

Gerald Vizenor's *Bearheart: The Heirship Chronicles*, first published in 1978 under the title *Darkness in St. Louis Bearheart*, is a startling tour de force where an ensemble of marginal characters engage in an epic journey through a futuristic American dystopia. The supply of gasoline is exhausted, and modern social institutions have disintegrated into mutated by-products of a social fusion. The containment field is gone, and nothing is as it was. Louis Owens aptly describes the novel as "a trickster narrative, a postapocalyptic allegory of mixedblood pilgrim clowns afoot in a world gone predictably mad" ("Afterword" 248).

The allegorical elements of the novel are quite pronounced. Readers are directed quickly to foregrounded episodes where social satire and political insight abound. The chapter that is set in the Bioavaricious Regional Word Hospital, an institution designed to "examine words where and when we find them in conflict" (166), and the chapters exploring how the liberators of Santa Fe become its new totalitarian rulers, resonate with contemporary and historical analogues. However, these social allegorical elements interweave with other mythological elements as well, such as transformations and epic journeys. With all the surprising actions of his characters and the social commentary, Vizenor's program is to disrupt the expectations of both audiences implied in his text. One key goal in that program is to bring the non-Native reader into the perceptual world of Native Americans. Vizenor explains, "I would like to imagine tribal experience for the non-Indian, whose frame of reference is very different from ours" (*Song* 165). In *Bearheart*, that also means the tribal experience of myth, not as an abstract body of stories but as an epistemological structuring of all experience. However, Vizenor's Native readers are also in store for a certain amount of upset and redirection.

Vizenor's task in reimagining a trickster narrative involves drawing upon a Native American oral tradition and placing it into contemporary novel form. Thus a fluid verbal field is put into a written form—a form that requires a certain degree of psychological unity and chronological causation. The novel draws upon a number of Western literary traditions including the gothic, the American Picaresque, the postmodern, and upon some specific works such as *Pilgrim's Progress*.[1] That readers, Native and non-Native, will approach this novel with certain expectations of literary realism is both a given and the starting point from which Vizenor must begin to shift the perspectives. However, one of Vizenor's primary tasks is to establish a representation of mythic awareness dynamic enough to excite meaning and yet static enough for the audience to recognize novelistic conventions, even if such conventions are in the process of being subverted. For Vizenor, any representation of the mythic falsifies it since its essence is fluid. However, a writer must present characters and events that can be comprehended. This contradiction in representation is expressed in all of Vizenor's work, and resolved in various ways in *Harold of Orange, Griever: An American Monkey King in China, The Trickster of Liberty: Tribal Heirs to a Wild Baronage, Interior Landscapes: Autobiographical Myths and Metaphors,* and *The Heirs of Columbus.*

Central to Vizenor's mediational goals for the implied Native and non-Native reader is the satirizing of terminal creeds—beliefs that are absolute and at a dead end. However, in this process readers can never be absolutely sure of who is being satirized at any one moment, because Vizenor's technique is to embed contradictions in the heart of his constructions. His is not, however, an attempt to avoid claims to absolute truth or uncontested meaning.[2] Rather, for Vizenor, contradiction is the essence of oral tradition in its emphasis on variation; its play between text and interpretation, its imaginative freedom, its subversion of absolute definitions of reality, and its ability to guide without demanding. The results of participation in an oral world view are imaginative survival and psychic healing—something both audiences need to appreciate. Terminal creeds lock the true believer into a moral system that lacks imaginative freedom. Contradiction frees cognition and opens up imagination—a process necessary for health and survival. Oral tradition, which flourishes in contradiction, is essential for survival, and Vizenor wants his fiction to have the healing power of oral stories. He proposes:

> Traditional tribal people imagine their social patterns and places on the earth, whereas anthropologists and historians invent tribal cultures and end mythic time. The differences between tribal imagination and social scientific invention are determined in world views: imagination is a state of being, a measure of personal courage; the invention of cultures is a material achievement through objective methodologies. To imagine the world is to be in the world; to invent the world with academic predications is to separate human experiences from the world . . . (*People* 27)

For Vizenor, to cease to imagine is to cease to grow. All cultural survival, Native and non-Native, depends on growth, so his fiction seeks to promote growth and balance through emphasizing the imaginative acts necessary for his implied readers to allow them to participate in his mythic satire.

Bearheart foregrounds this struggle against the terminal

creeds that impede imaginative and cultural survival. Ruoff notes that through his Chippewa background, Vizenor has learned how "myths and stories are essential to Indian survival and renewal" ("Woodland" 24). However, as he tries to place insights from Native oral tradition into contemporary fiction, mythic satire informs the effort.

Primary among *Bearheart*'s insights is what Maureen Keady calls the blurring of good and evil, the idea "that truths and falsehoods are so often spoken from the same mouths and within the same sentences" (62). In the world of the novel, morals are not as black and white as we would feel comfortable believing. This contradictory world is what Vizenor sees in the trickster narrative. He would have his readers experience the world in a position that is between absolute terms and between myth and reality, letting the contradictions illuminate each other and layer our understanding and perception. Explains Vizenor, "I choose words intentionally because they have established multiple symbolic meanings, and sometimes I put them in place so that they're in contradiction, so that you can read it several ways. . . . I work on the most obvious binaries . . . but I shift them to multiple meanings" (qtd. in Coltelli 175).

While we learn from this novel about terminal creeds, we also discover a perceptual path back to balance and psychic healing. One of the most important terminal creeds to be deconstructed is that of the Indian, a romantic concept invented by European/Americans for their own needs. Natives and non-Natives who believe in this conception of themselves are out of balance. Owens observes, "*Bearheart* is such a liberation, an attempt to free us from the romantic entrapments, to liberate the imagination" (*Other* 231). As it contradicts the implied reader's concept of Indian, it frees Indian identity. While this may be an important action for an implied non-Native reader, it is vital for the implied Native reader in need of healing and balance and for Native social survival in general. For Vizenor, myth's essential role in Native survival is more than a set of laws or a coded set of instructions. It is at the very heart of how to think, how to imagine: it is the essence of world view. Jahner links this concept with Vizenor's goal as a writer when she concludes, "The power of Vizenor's belief that the oral tradition stays alive in the distances between contraries and that these distances are fields of vision has been the driving force behind all of his narrative experimentation" ("Cultural" 26).[3]

Bearheart does not exactly place us in a mythic world; rather it places us between myth and reality. Traditional stories are used to reveal wisdom and world view, but they are also used to narrate the actions of particular characters. Contemporary society is extrapolated and transformed into myth and epic, but the realistic details of everyday reality are chronicled at the same time. Alan Velie has clearly established how the novel is "anchored in a world whose time and place are familiar" ("Trickster" 132). In the novel, the interstate highways, fast food restaurants, scarred cities, and trailer ruins are peopled with tricksters, travelers, and an evil gambler. In this in-between world, both implied readers' expectations of myth and reality can be placed in contradiction and thus liberated. Part of Vizenor's multiple sense of meaning is to have the reader experience an important element of Native world view rather than be lectured about it. The reader can stand in between, waver, and be transformed.

For the implied Native reader, more appreciative of Native world view, Vizenor encourages a new perception of the contradictions essential to oral narrative. This implied reader must perceive how myth and oral tradition are translated into the new context of writing. Vizenor's belief that oral narratives require visual imagination is embodied in his fictions, which he refers to as *word cinemas*. The implied Native reader must then perceive the visual in written rather than oral form. Jahner notes how Vizenor's writing can forge new connections between the written and oral, the modern and traditional. To this end, he uses:

memories of tribal tradition, all aspects of it, the linguistic and nonlinguistic, all of which are bound to each other and to present time and setting through the way people use their capacity to link what they *see* in the present to what they remember in the past. This capacity to link past and present is essentially metaphorical. Words that maintain those links, whether oral or written, keep a person in touch with the fundamental meaning of the creation myth which is a mode of connection between the past and the present. ("Cultural" 24–25)

Bringing the traditional vision into the modern world is a creative act, one that could even help reunite an individual with a sustaining culture. Such contradictions and creations open up the implied Native reader to other contradictions, such as the elements of a fluid, dynamic, even contradictory definition of Indian identity. As the novel opens, the mixed-blood Bearheart insists that the AIM-type activist read the text. Vizenor's narrative frame initiates a deconstruction of the implied Native reader's identity, asserting the necessity of abandoning a static definition of that identity, one that victimizes Indian people and threatens cultural survival. As a journalist and community organizer who has aimed many a text at Native audiences, Vizenor has a clear idea of his implied Native reader and of the kind of active reading he hopes to encourage.

Essential for both readers, but especially for the implied non-Native reader, is the kind of reality evoked in the novel—one where myth has come to life. Oral traditions are once again central to man and woman's experience of the world, but now the new trickster narratives are experienced because readers are placed inside a mythic world. While many of the familiar structures of modern life are no longer functional, the interstate highways remain, becoming roads to knowledge. The wandering ensemble of pilgrims finds renewed value in the old sources, family and community, and renewed meaning in dreams. Of this world, Vizenor writes in *Bearheart*:

Oral traditions were honored. Families welcomed good tellers of stories, the wandering historians of follies and tragedies. Readers and writers were seldom praised but the traveling raconteurs were one form of the new shamans on the interstates. Facts and the need for facts had died with newspapers and politics. Nonfacts were more believable. The listeners traveled with the tellers through the same frames of time and place. The telling was in the listening. When the sun had set travelers and moths were drawn to the flames. Stories were told about fools and tricksters and human animals. Myths became the center of meaning again. (162)

As myth becomes the center of meaning in the reality of the text, it also becomes the center of meaning for both implied readers. However, these myths are "stories of folly and tragedy" and ones that the reader must experience personally if telling is to become listening. Tricksters, fools, and animal humans abound in the novel, subverting the realistic conventions of character and introducing a high level of contradiction through their wildly imaginative stories and actions.

The textual path of Vizenor's mediation leads him to structure an implied reader's experience so that nonfacts become more believable than facts—a reversal that is contrary to Western epistemology. The text moves between perceptions that are both familiar and unfamiliar. According to Hayden White, discourse is always as much about the restructuring of perception as it is about the supposed subject. White sheds light on Vizenor's method in his description of the mediative process as a kind of discourse that moves between "received encodations of experience" and the other elements that refuse "incorporation into conventional notions of 'reality,' 'truth,' or 'possibility'" (4). As an alternate way of encoding reality, mythic perception might be alien to the non-Native reader. In order to travel with the tellers through the same frames of time and place, such a reader must be instructed in the way myth conveys meaning. Yet a static representation of mythic thinking that freezes its subject in realistic conventions would never successfully accomplish a mediative and epistemological goal of altering the way the reader creates meaning and bringing him or her into the "mode of connection" of the creation myth. As Vizenor writes in his essay "Trickster Discourse," "Verisimilitude is the appearance of realities; mythic verism is discourse, a critical concordance of narrative voices, and a narrative realism that is more than mimesis or a measure of what is believed to be natural in the world" (190). Thus to follow Vizenor's mythic restructuring is to explore the discourse as contradiction, as a concordance of voices, and to abandon verisimilitude and facts for a new narrative realism that is more than a reflection of what we think to be natural.

Richard Rorty in his study of representation and epistemology, *Philosophy and the Mirror of Nature*, confirms that "as long as knowledge is conceived of as accurate representing—as the mirror of nature . . . such accuracy requires a theory of privileged representations, ones which are automatically and intrinsically accurate" (170). Opposite to mythic perception for Vizenor are terminal creeds—those privileged representations that cut off all narrative conversation and humor. Terminal creeds cannot be overcome with confrontation by other more accurate representation, but rather with discourse, with conversation, with countering privileged representations with other representations, some of which might also claim absolute truth. However, both implied readers will realize that no one representation can subsume another. In Vizenor's terms, the characters and the readers must remain "between." They must waver and continue to transform. Rorty continues, "Once conversation replaces confrontation, the notion of the Mirror of Nature can be discarded. . . . If we see knowledge as a matter of conversation and of social practice, rather than as an attempt to mirror nature, we will not be likely to envisage a metapractice which will be the critique of all possible forms of social practice" (170–71). Vizenor's mediative text attempts to expand the implied reader's struggle against terminal creeds or against what he or she formerly believed to be natural in the world, the received encodations.

In search of this new narrative realism, this concordance of narrative voices, Vizenor allows discourse to dominate the reader's experience of the novel. Many examples of mythic perception and participation, a process involving conversational discourse, can be found in the novel. Vizenor uses mythic characters, such as the Evil Gambler[4] and Changing Woman but alters their function so that the implied readers must interrogate the meaning of these characters. A powerful example is Vizenor's incorporation of what has been termed the *Dog Husband* story. Stith Thompson refers to it as a story originating in the North Pacific coast and Alaska and spreading to the western plains and down to California (*Folktale* 355).[5] The story is first introduced in the novel when Proude Cedarfair tells it at the last dinner of the starving priests of the Sacred Order of Gay Minikins. In Proude's version, the girl who has taken the dog as lover flees the rage and fear of her family and village when her lover is killed. Aided by shaman crows, she gives birth to five puppies. When two are killed and eaten by humans, she leads the remaining ones to kill sleeping humans. The humans learn from the owls and crows that this evil is occurring because of their history of shunning animals. The humans reform and begin to love animals so much that they start to die of hunger. The animals become fat and selfish, and the crows become disgusted with the "terminal creeds of the humans" (63): first their absolute love of themselves, and then their absolute love of animals. They convince the girl to let her puppies become human, and then she leads the humans to a new age of harmony where they love both animals and themselves. This paradise is eventually interrupted by white men who destroy the bond. The crows then turn tribal children into mongrels to save them from being devoured. Slowly the white men's hearts are eaten up with evil because they have shunned animals.

Proude uses the story to counteract the Minikins' passive

desire to starve to death. They have made a religion, a terminal creed, out of savoring the last meal, the last taste of life. Proude's story reveals how beliefs can allow one to be devoured, physically or spiritually, and that such consumption is a birthplace of evil. Vizenor adds to this basic insight a criticism of Western civilization's separation from the animal/spiritual world—from what Vizenor calls "the wisdom of the shaman crows" (62).

The story again appears when Inawa Biwide tells it to Lilith Mae Farrier. His version is similar to Proude's except that he tells how after the mother is ostracized, she grows angry with her puppies because the clown crows have taught them through humor and dance to assume human form. However, when the crows chastise her for her mean attitude toward humans, she agrees to let the puppies become human. She teaches them to be great hunters, and they aid the starving villagers who drove their mother out. The puppies never tell anyone about their origin, and Biwide concludes, "The crows know which of our lives are birds and animals and human" (94). His version points to the unity of animals and humans in nature such as the ancient stories often explore. More specifically, it responds to Lilith Mae's love/hate relationship with her dogs and with the stepfather who sexually abused her. She has come to Bishop Parasimo's cathedral tunnel "to confess her sexual sins, hoping to recover passion in her passionless emotions" (78). The story reveals that goodness comes from an understanding of our essentially mutable nature and the intimate secrets of our origins (which are mysterious and only to be discovered on a spiritual plane). These two versions interrogate each other's construction of the story's meaning, while pointing to different perspectives on the unity or disunity of the animal/human world.

More contradictions develop when the telling of the story fuses with the living of the story as readers learn of Lilith Mae Farrier's relations to the dogs on the reservation. She feeds the mongrels who follow her around the reservation. School officials on the reservation take sexual advantage of her, and she is driven off the reservation with only two dogs left. The boxers then become literally her lovers. This more objectified version of the story, which moves to different levels of narrative reality, confronts the other versions that were distanced in the text as myths. Such a confrontation generates the present reality of the text—a reality where the listener Lilith Mae travels with the teller, Inawa Biwide. The effect on both implied readers is to see the stories as discourse, the polyvocal play of narrative that Vizenor describes as mythic verism. Since Proude's version of the story has the reservation children turning into mongrels, Lilith's copulation with dogs literally embraces mythic tribal transformers. Indeed, later in the novel, the mongrels accompanying the journey even prove to be shaman healers (156).

Each audience's terminal creeds are contradicted. Implied Native readers, who believed that animals were sacred, would have humans starve. If they believe, as Belladonna Darwin-Winter Catcher did, in some absolute difference of Indian values based on blood and heritage, then they create an isolating narcissism. These romantic terminal creeds leave no room for relationship and conversation. Non-native readers, locked into a view of human nature as essentially fallen, depraved and evil, and also a view of animals as inferior beings, would want the humans' hearts to be eaten up with evil. The oral narratives and the novel itself both seek a common ground: between good and evil, between past and present, between myth and reality, between oral and written, between different telling of the same story.

The multifaceted interweavings of actions, people and transformations allow *Bearheart* to take a mediative stance that moves beyond the privileged representations of science, especially social science and its textual analogue, literary Realism. The implied reader is encouraged to identify with an epistemological perspective, mythic in its assumptions. As conversation and discourse, the novel shifts meaning production away from terminal creeds of an author, with their one-dimensional allegories and privileged representations, and onto a reader who has many perspectives. Vizenor contends that this shift is essential in understanding Native American literatures because they are "tribal discourse, more discourse. The oral and written narratives are language games, comic discourse rather than mere responses to colonialist demands or social science theories" ("Postmodern" 4). When implied readers are less concerned with the logical consistencies of one account of the story, or with whether it can be taken as true and factual, they become more open to the language game of discourse. White explains that the function of such discourse is to "*constitute* the ground whereon to decide *what shall count as a fact* in the matters under consideration and to determine *what mode of comprehension* is best suited to the understanding of the facts thus constituted" (3).

This reconstitution necessitates revising accepted romantic representations of Native Americans. Undoubtedly some of the sexual violence in the novel serves the iconoclastic function of negating stereotypes of the noble Indian. Indeed, Vizenor often refers to the agonistic imagination that tribal narratives generate, and the sexual violence of his narratives would force some agonistic responses from readers.

Still, central to an understanding of Vizenor's work is the analysis of the contradictions inherent in a textual representation of mythic awareness and in the mediative positioning of implied readers. Vizenor supplies us with some insight into his goals when he writes: "The active reader implies the author, imagines narrative voices, inspires characters, and salutes tribal tricksters in a comic discourse; an erotic motion under the words absolves the separation between minds and bodies" (*The Trickster of Liberty* xi). As the active reader enters the reality that the text constitutes, imagination gives life to the characters and that gives life to the discourse. The active reader implies the author since the reader's role is the one assigned by Vizenor. As readers begin to participate in the contradictions, they must create an implied author as the source of these contradictions if they are to establish meaning. The authorial role is buoyed by an erotic motion that is comic. For Vizenor, comedy can be equated with that which is adaptive and which enlightens without trying to transform. The motion is erotic since it comes from the life-sustaining forces of Eros and the desire for unification. The comic erotic motion of the imagination heals the mind/body split, encouraging imaginative capacity and curing the belief in terminal creeds that define identity and culture.

Vizenor is convinced that the active reader's participation makes him a player in the language game rather than an observer. As the author weighs and plays with the ironies, cultural myths, and social metaphors, he creates competing perspectives, bringing the effort to find meaning as constituted by discourse to a central position for both audiences. Discourse as conversation is created. Vizenor explains, "The active readers become obverse tricksters, the waver of a coin in a tribal striptease. . . . To imagine the tribal trickster is to relume human unities; colonial surveillance, monologues, and racial separations are overturned in discourse" (*The Trickster of Liberty* ix–x).

As Proude and Inawa fly with the vision bears into the fourth world, the reader flies into vision as well. Evil and death have been sidestepped thorugh a discourse that has altered the reader's creation of meaning. Nothing is the same except the sign of the trickster that dallies momentarily on each of the pilgrims and then flies off to a new world. Monologues, terminal creeds, and privileged representations are deconstructed. Mythic verism becomes the only criterion of accuracy. Ultimately Vizenor's tricksters outwit evil but never kill it because humans must learn to live imaginatively with contradictions: "Evil revenge is blind and cannot be appeased by the living. The tricksters and warrior clowns have stopped more evil violence with their wit than have lovers with their lust and fools with the power and rage." (*Bearheart* 15).

Much of the content of the novel is intended to encourage the active reader and to constitute mythic verism. For implied Native readers there is the satire of contemporary American society, the BIA, the Indian activists, the tribal officials, and romantic conceptions of shamans. As they imagine the narrative voices, the implied Native readers establish the contradictions that allow them to become active readers. Also, the use of oral narratives, especially involving trickster characters, provides a familiar frame of appreciation, but that frame is quickly revised and contradicted since the tricksters are involved in extraordinary and often undesirable actions. Of the trickster Vizenor claims, "More than a magnanimous teacher and transformer, the trickster is capable of violence, deceptions, and cruelties: the realities of human imperfections" (*People* 4). Mythic verism humanizes the trickster as well as the pilgrims in the novel who have trickster qualities.[6] A cosmic and mythic sense of justice prevails as characters die in manners fitting to their beliefs in terminal creeds. However, the Native reader is asked to perceive these characters in creative rather than religious terms, drawing upon the imagination and not cultural belief.

Much of the humanization of myth influences implied non-Native readers as well, though for them, such myths have never been a matter of belief or an article of faith. It may be difficult at first for these readers to recognize such humanizing because, in keeping with oral narrative, it does not go into an elaborate psychology to explain motivation. Actions define meaning, and often things just seem to happen, for Vizenor believes that chance is "a very important element of storytelling. Things just happen, you cannot account for them . . . " ("Interview" 107). Robbed of much of the linearity and causality expected, the implied non-Native reader has to place greater emphasis on the dreams and visions of the characters. He or she can participate in the transformations and become an active, imaginative reader. Such contradictions as the sex reversals of Pio Wissakodewinini and the metamask transformations of Bishop Omax Parasimo prevent the reader from being incorporated easily into an existing system of moral judgment. The contradictions in the characters, their actions, and even their natures encourage a more active reader who can harmonize the dynamic perspectives of mythic verism. From this perspective, the transformations of Proude Cedarfair and Inawa Biwide become logical occurrences in a world where dreams and visions contain more truth than facts.[7]

An aim of Vizenor's trickster narrative is, as Owens says, "to free Indian identity from the epic, absolute past that insists upon stasis and tragedy for Native Americans" (*Other* 231). Multiple narratives help broaden the received definitions of identity while deconstructing static formulations. Clearly the mythical transformations of Proude and Inawa define their mythic identities. However, previous to those transformations, all the characters have participated in fictional versions of mythic narratives, such as the struggle with the Evil Gambler, which was taken from oral narratives and transformed into fiction. They have been moved from sociological and psychological definitions to more oral, more Native senses of identity that include mythic and communal elements. Even the dogs and crows who accompany the wanderers take on mythic roles as seers, guides, and shaman healers.

The communal narrative establishes Proude in the role of a shaman healer. As a spiritual guide, his function is to bring each character into balance in the third world. His task is not to escort each pilgrim to the vision window in Pueblo Bonito, but to help each find the place where he or she belongs, where they can balance their good and evil, their emotions and their terminal beliefs, their lives and their deaths. As such he is committed to life and change. When he gives away one of the medicine bundles he carries, the pilgrims are shocked, but he responds, "The power of the human spirit is carried in the heart not in histories and materials. . . . Good spirits soar with the birds and the sun not in secret bundles" (218–19). He takes them as far as their hearts will go and lets them find balance.

In the novel's fictional world of real myth, sociological definitions of identity are deconstructed so that characters can find their places, their points of balance. Proude is the last leader of the cedar nation, but this social role is abandoned during the journey. He turns to "the cleverness of crows and the visions and ceremonial powers of the bears" (16). However other characters also give up social definitions of identity that are tied to the decaying modern world. For example, Lilith Mae is no longer the teacher; Justice Pardone Cozener abandons the world of the tribal bigbellies; Bishop Omax Parasimo leaves his religious position. In the world of the novel, all societies have disintegrated and in this disintegration, Vizenor is able to satirize Native and non-Native social stances and definitions of identity that are locked into terminal creeds. He and his readers become practitioners of socioacupuncture.

Vizenor provides psychological information about most of his characters; however, the intent is less to explain motivation than to satirize social constructions. Sir Cecil Staples's childhood of kidnapping and of ingesting toxic chemicals says more about modern American society than it does about his mythic identity as the Evil Gambler. The same is true for Lilith Mae, who was molested by her stepfather as a child and who takes an animal lover as an adult. Only Proude and Rosina seem to exist in actions and in dreams without the hinderance of psychological background. For Vizenor, these contradictions between the expected psychological motivation and realized social analysis are essential in positioning both implied readers so that imagination can flourish. Psychology can easily become a terminal creed, and mythic verism requires disbelief. As implied readers become active readers, they perceive the conversations that define Vizenor's tribal discourse. Thus they can "relume human unities" in a world of imaginative reality and escape the third world that has turned evil "with contempt for living and fear of death" (5).

What Did You See?

Wind From an Enemy Sky

◆

D'Arcy McNickle spent years revising his novel, *Wind from an Enemy Sky*, in order to reflect his experience in white/ Indian affairs. Some of that experience was gained under the auspices of the BIA, some with pan-tribal organizations like the American Indian Development fund and the National Congress of American Indians, and some in a personal capacity as critic, editor, and teacher. He wrote in 1976, "The present draft of the novel is the last of many versions of the story I attempted over a twenty year period. I experienced many interruptions in the writing, and each interruption seemed to result in a new approach to the material. . . . About two years ago I returned to the manuscript and re-wrote the entire script in about six months" (qtd. in Purdy 106).

John Purdy perceptively discusses some of the revisions in the novel's development, and in the consideration of these revisions, one thing seems clear: McNickle tried with each draft to refocus his message while he reconstituted the text. The interruptions from novel writing gave McNickle new insights into how best to construct a text to move his readers. Certainly how his audience reacted to the text was of utmost importance to McNickle. However, his purpose was also mediative: McNickle aimed to re-educate both Native and non-Native readers so that they could better understand each other's cultural codes. *Wind From an Enemy Sky* was his last and best attempt to illuminate the cognitive structures in this cross-cultural dynamic, reflecting years of personal experience and his refined literary talent.

The role of each implied reader can be deduced by following the shifts in textual perspectives and by identifying the cultural discourse fields surrounding each reader's role. As a mediative enterprise then, *Wind From an Enemy Sky* must engage not only the reader's present perception but respond to the discourse field upon which the text builds because it is the source of those perceptions. Reading the novel then could become a cross-cultural event. As both implied readers become aware of the discourse field of the other, they begin Bakhtin's ideological translation and come to an appreciation of the goals of such discourse. The readers also begin to perceive the intersubjectivity or intertextuality of the novel's discourse. A useful way of discussing this dimension is to apply in a cultural context Donald Bialostosky's formulation of the "dialogic conversation" in order to understand the nature of the discourse field that each new text advances.[1]

I would contend that we can see in *Wind From an Enemy Sky* at least two cultural conversations and a dual set of textual and cultural goals. While we may assume that readers can easily reconstruct how McNickle appreciated the cultural conversation of the dominant culture in the early 1970s, we may have more trouble identifying the outlines of the cultural conversation addressed to the implied Native reader. The trend of much of the research on Native American Literature has been to seek out the cultural referents from specific tribal traditions in order to understand the cultural conversation in the narrative. Indeed some critics suggest that we should examine writers primarily in the context of their tribal traditions. According to this perspective, Leslie Silko's work is seen only as contributing to Laguna Literature and Simon Ortiz's work only as contributing to Acoma Literature. While there is some value to this approach, the methodology does not really delineate the ways in which the discourse of a text may be addressed to a non-Laguna or non-Acoma Native audience as well. And for *Wind From an Enemy Sky* such a cultural approach would yield only limited insights, for though McNickle drew on his tribal experience for some background, the book addressed a pan-tribal audience in ways that none of his other novels did. In other words, I would argue that McNickle used his appreciation of Native thought and values to create a pan-tribal cognitive system for the novel rather than to promote Cree, Salish, or any other specifically tribal outlook.

Starting from the supposition that McNickle addressed both a non-Native and a Native reader, it is fruitful to explore the nature of those readers as implied in the roles assigned to each by McNickle. I draw here on Iser's construction of the implied reader but with my own modifications. Iser does not take into theoretical consideration the existence of two separate implied readers, one with a Western value system and another capable of applying both Native and Western values to events in the text. By defining the cognitive position of his readers in relation to their appropriate discourse fields, McNickle establishes a starting point for them. He then positions each to move through the shifting textual perspectives on events in the novel. As implied readers move through the text, they develop a new perception of the meaning of the text and a new way of thinking about the world around them.

McNickle viewed his mainstream American implied reader as someone who knew little of actual Native American life and thought, but who had some interest in the Indian. McNickle obviously knew he needed to break the stereotype of the stoic Native traditionalist obstructing the benefits of progress for no good reason. For years the author had aimed to negate stereotypes in his ethno-historical writing and in his previous novels. His approach in *Wind* was to define "the map of the mind" (125) of his Native American characters, or as John Purdy puts it, "to attract his readers into his primary lesson: an understanding of how and why, the Indians react as they do" (128).[2] To show why Indians reacted as they did, McNickle condensed various elements of Native American cultures and sought to establish this map for a non-Native implied reader; moreover, he included in *Wind* some overtly political discourse, directing it toward the non-Native reader who lived during the social upheaval of the 1960s.

During those years, the counterculture resurrected many romantic images of the Indian. Frederick Turner gives perhaps the best outline of white romantic thinking about Indians in his Introduction to *The Portable North American Indian Reader*. Turner identified six essential 1960s beliefs about the Indian: (1) he was the original ecologist; (2) he was the original communist with a small "c"; (3) he was not an aggressive fighter; (4) he was a natural democrat; (5) he was noncompetitive; and (6) he was wise because he was prescientific (10).

But by 1974, the image of the peace-loving, communal, spiritual Indian was tarnished by the violence of AIM and Wounded Knee. Many liberal readers were taken aback. In the early seventies *Black Elk Speaks* had reached innumerable readers and brought awareness of injustice while reinforcing a sense of Indian nobility. As McNickle finished the last draft of *Wind*, interest in and confusion about Indians was at a high point. His narrative, set in a past era, was meant to explain something of the cultural differences that kept the dominant culture from understanding Native Americans. This temporal distancing allowed him to avoid a defense of AIM-type violence; he still argued though that suppression of Native rights would inevitably lead to violence.

In 1973 McNickle published a revised version of *The Indian Tribes of the United States: Ethnic and Cultural Survival*. He used its introduction to address the 1972 takeover of the BIA and the events at Wounded Knee in the spring of 1973. Like a good historian, McNickle advised his readers of the persistent pattern of federal usurpation of Native American rights and the specifically odious Eisenhower years of termination and relocation; he then linked the present violence and the divisiveness created in Indian communities with the detrimental effect of outside interference in the internal social dynamic of change, even if that interference was with the best of good will. He concluded:

> Older Indians had tried to live with that reality, seeing no way around it, hence their unwillingness to challenge the forces around them. If they waited and talked quietly among themselves, perhaps the forces would wither away and they would not have to surrender what was left.
> So the anger of the young was in part directed at the old men of the tribe, but that was anger within the family. The real targets were the men in far places, of good faith or bad, who still thought themselves as the only proper source of Indian well being.
> It now seems likely after Washington and Wounded Knee, that anger will hang in the air, like a combustible vapor, for some time to come. Indian Americans need assurance that riots are not essential preliminaries for purposeful talk. (xiii)

McNickle's literary texts are suffused with social insights. It is not a large step to see how this political discourse becomes dramatized in Bull's initial unwillingness to challenge the forces around him and his hope that they will wither away or in Jim's anger with the old men of the tribe who were holding the people back. McNickle's viewpoint is apparent in many passages, such as when Iron Child concludes that Henry Jim was not to blame for the quarrel that has split the tribe, but rather that the white intrusion is to blame and that the tribe reacted as it did because it was "losing out" (84) to the whites. Pell's actions in constructing the dam and in offering the gold statue not only characterize him as the type of reformer with which McNickle must have dealt, but also reveal him to be one of those "men in far places" who think they know what is best for the Indian. While in the previously cited passage, McNickle was speaking of anger in the air following Wounded Knee, *Wind From an Enemy Sky* also expresses anger: white anger over the killing and the perceived backwardness of the Indians, and Indian anger over continued white domination and oppression. In the tragedy at the end, Indian anger finally explodes. McNickle hopes that riots are not essential, yet *Wind* can be read as implying that they might prepare the ground for purposeful political talk, if only to discuss the causes of violence. This foregrounding of overtly political Native perceptions introduces the non-Native implied reader to the causes of Indian anger and frustration. Moreover, the sense of the inadequacy of non-Native understanding of Indian thought (best exemplified by Pell) keeps the implied non-Native reader from rushing into a specific solution. Implied non-Native readers are led to see that the "real targets" are those like themselves who come with solutions to Indian problems.

One can find a number of explicitly political passages in McNickle's writings and correspondence since his insights and attitudes were honed over decades of work at the cross-cultural barricades. But it is also important for an understanding of McNickle's text to focus on the ways the novel engages non-Native discourse of the 1970s on a cultural as well as political basis.

Throughout the novel there is a conscious effort to contrast sources of knowledge, senses of the past, and ideas of justice, to name only a few areas. This mediating exploration of epistemology and cultural values is embedded to evoke a greater sense of tolerance and understanding in the non-Native reader, while validating the Native world view for the implied Native reader. There are many sections in which McNickle directly addresses his readers, adopting a position similar to oral storytellers who will insert direct interpretation into their tellings. These intrusions serve to hold the non-Native reader off from making quick conclusions about the meaning of events. For example, he reminds us how difficult it is "to translate one man's life to another's" (26), or he comments that "ends are never seen in the beginnings" (238). Rafferty's realization that he must judge others by their fitness to their world, and that the Little Elk Indians have a different map of mind (125), makes him more willing to listen before he acts. Pell's insight that Native ideas are rational, though they work from "different data and a different order of reality" (210) is similarly enlightening for him. However, Pell's assumptions are fundamentally wrong and when translated into action, they precipitate tragedy. Pell's and Rafferty's revelations negate stereotypes without acknowledging that Native American world view is something that can be learned by non-Natives.

These authorial intrusions and moments of illumination by key non-Native characters create some elbow room for Native culture and thought. They reveal acceptable attitudes for implied non-Native readers to identify with, but the cautionary quality of these attitudes, and the fact that they are foregrounded in the text, encourage the non-Native reader to hold off the construction of the meaning from that which has passed over the event horizon of the text.

Other sections acknowledge a history of non-Native discourse about Natives that has not included Native voices. McNickle reinstates the Native voice by adopting the storyteller's stance and allowing the character Henry Jim to do so too. Jim cannot shape an action in the present without telling a story from the past, a story "carried back to the beginnings." He explains, "Today talks in yesterday's voice. . . . The white man must hear yesterday's voice" (28). To shape the actions of today, McNickle's novel tells a story of the past, of an imaginary Indian tribe at the time of a reform administration and its great dam building projects similar to the ones the United States had in the 1930s. As he does so, he reestablishes the non-Native discourse field about Indians, especially through characters like Marshal Sid Grant, Adam Pell, and Reverend Stephen Welles. Reverend Welles voices the bitter conviction of the failed missionary: "The Indian people start from origins about which we speculate but know next to nothing. . . . The Indian is anti-civilization! . . . If there were two humanities, I'd say he is with the other party. . . . They will not abandon the old and the familiar, if left to themselves. They can only choose what they have always known, and that choice means extinction for them" (51–52). These convictions express the old belief that whites must kill the Indian to save the man, for only by wrenching the Indian from his culture and forcing the adoption of mainstream American culture, can he survive.

In contrast to this late nineteenth-century and early twentieth-century rhetoric is the discourse of reformers such as Adam Pell. Pell, the romanticist, who has made a hobby of Indians, has modern progressive plans. He believes that the Indians are capable of being empowered. He says of the Peruvian Indians, "When opportunity came to them they were quite capable of adopting new ideas" (145). However, the opportunity is created by one rich non-Native who has a vision of how to better the lives of the oppressed Natives. He initiates a plan of social reform devised by himself. Through the concerted actions of one individual, Carlos, "an extraordinary human community" develops where "people were discovering what it meant to be human" (148). Pell wants his actions to live up to this dream. He sees something better than wardship for the Indians and acknowledges the failure of previous interfering plans, but still must try to meddle to "restore something of what they lost through my carelessness" (234). He acts under the reformist belief that his values can be transferred to another group of people.

These threads of discourse form the contemporary historical and cultural conversation about Indians and their relationship to European America. McNickle lets the character Rafferty learn and grow through his responses to the frontier, missionary, and reformist discourse about Indians. As he does so, he assumes the role implied for the non-Native reader. Rafferty's introduction to Native life, his reasonable approach, his growing awareness of the externally created problems of the Little Elk Indians, and his sincere desire to help, give the non-Native readers a model for how they might respond to the text. Yet even Rafferty does not embody the restrained role that McNickle wishes contemporary America would adopt. As Rafferty, the in-text substitute reader, dies, so does the non-Native reader who started the book. The specific constellation of attitudes of that self must also die so that the cultural conversation can evolve past even reformist thinking. McNickle wants the non-Native implied reader to hear the voice of yesterday before advocating the actions of today.

As the non-Native discourse field about Natives is explored, countered, and expanded, we can note one of the primary formal elements through which this mediational goal takes shape. What starts out as a murder mystery quickly changes into the type of mystery known as a procedural since we know who is the killer, and only the questions of whether they will find him, and why he did it remain. Yet after awhile it is hard for most readers to sustain a strong desire to take Pock-face to trial and hang him. It seems ever so much more reasonable that the Indian system of justice should prevail and the two families should get together and settle the problem. Sid Grant proves to be an arrogant, intrusive detective. Because of his smug and superior frontier manner and his automatic assumption of Indian culpability, non-Native implied readers start to lose not only identification with him, but with the system of justice he represents. The scene in Rafferty's office, which brings all the principals together, is a perfect parody of the murder mystery convention where the detective assembles the suspects to reveal the murderer. However in *Wind*, the murderer unexpectedly confesses, and nobody knows exactly what to do about it. The Indians expect that they must immediately respond so as to compensate the family. The whites want Pock-Face to remain quiet. They are uncomfortable, expecting impersonal legal proceedings which however, as Bull says, will make everyone angry. The two perceptions of justice are juxtaposed in a convention of non-Native discourse concerning the murder mystery. The non-Native belief that revealing the murderer will lead to justice is thwarted. In the conventions of the murder mystery, the revelation of the murderer brings closure and a sense of understanding, but here only more questions are created. When faced with people holding different cultural attitudes about the individual's responsibility toward society and the spiritual world, the Native concept of justice highlights the inadequacy of the Western concept of justice. More importantly, that implied reader is pushed to examine how he or she has made sense of the death and the events leading up to it. The non-Native reader is encouraged to reexamine the events of the text that have slipped over the event horizon in order to understand how his or her sense of meaning has developed.

The Native implied reader might feel that a Native world view is validated, but the murder is sufficiently random so as to not fit comfortably into a Native sense of personal justice. He or she is encouraged to examine how this Native sense of justice fits into a new world. The mystery for this reader involves the question of whether Feather Boy will be returned. Epistemologically it concerns the significance of a medicine bundle: Why is it so important and how can it influence the life of a people? On a more practical social level, the question becomes: what will the Little Elk Indians do if it is not returned? By the end of the novel, the cultural conversation about Native Americans is engaged and redirected, first into a contemporary discussion about violence and then into a validation of a different world view. With this textual shift in perspective, the conventions of discourse about Natives and the Western system of justice are appropriated for decidedly Native goals.

Of course key determinants in all readers' responses are the questions asked of Antoine in the beginning that reverberate in the middle and at the end of the novel: What did you see? What did you learn? What will you remember? (8, 116, 238) Both Native and non-Native implied readers must answer those questions for themselves. The final meanings of the text then are not in the novel but in the readers' appreciation as they take this voice of the past into present action and insight.

The non-Native readers are encouraged to conclude that their actions can hurt both non-Natives and Natives, that cultural misunderstanding too easily leads to tragedy, and that they need to respect Native conclusions and be slow to interfere even when they think they see the right answer. The questions are foregrounded in much the same way as Iser describes the wandering perspective. While initially they are associated with the narrator, they quickly become internalized as questions in Antoine's mind. With the death of Rafferty, the non-Native reader is guided to shift his or her perspective to that of McNickle, the storyteller, and ask what Antoine has learned. However, as these questions are directed to the implied readers, their answers are the *raison d'être* for the text. This attempt to shift the reader's perception to a more Native perspective is made more explicit in McNickle's nonfiction prose where he often argues for an "enduring policy of self-determined cultural pluralism" (*Native* 169) toward Indians.

Through the authorial intrusions, the contrasting chapters, the death of the non-Native implied reader in the text (via Rafferty), the parody of the mystery form, and the use of questions, McNickle embeds a high degree of self-reflexiveness, guiding the non-Native implied reader to view the novel as a narrative whose meaning he or she must puzzle out. The authorial comments and questions also create a tone that is personal in a way reminiscent of oral storytelling. In a sense, McNickle is adopting a mediational strategy common in traditional Native oral narratives, perhaps even encouraging non-Native implied readers to acknowledge an unexpected form of knowledge derived from storytelling. They are directed to adopt a world view where dreams reveal truth and a song can keep a person alive, where stories from the past provide the meaning for events of the present. They must live in that world view, if only for a moment. Consequently, new elements have entered the cultural conversation in the process of redirecting the discourse about Natives.

McNickle's storytelling also creates a mediative frame with which Native readers might be familiar. The power of songs, visions, and traditional stories might reinforce certain cultural precognitive positions since the voice of the past speaks to today's world. Moreover, the questions asked of Antoine obviously serve to focus the perspective for the implied Native reader. They require not only a reaffirmation of tribal values and an appreciation of injustice already present in most Native readers, but also a historical, political, and scientific analysis, one that is more than an emotional and cultural response. At first the Little Elk Indians think that the whites are awkward and unable to survive (135), but eventually they realize that though they are "a people without respect . . . they managed to get what they wanted" (131). While Jim moves to adopt white ways, Bull withdraws to "a time when people waited and did nothing" (133). Native implied readers are encouraged to analyze change, identity, and community, not just respond. The death of Bull, a viewpoint character for a Native implied reader with activist tendencies, pushes that reader to calculate the dynamics of isolation and violence. Bull's move from his confined world where he saw that "death always waited beyond the camp circle" (93) to his violent response at the end of the novel reminds the Native reader that cultural continuity is not synonymous with isolation and that reaction is a victim's strategy.

The parameters of the cultural conversation to which McNickle saw this book responding are delineated in his other writing from the 1970s. McNickle's revision of *Indians and Other Americans* in 1970 offers an insight into his implied Native reader. The 1959 edition of *Indians and Other Americans* ended with an appeal for a four point plan similar to the one Congress approved for Iran. The 1970 edition concluded with the promotion of an identity that would be pan-Indian as opposed to tribal specific, pointing to the political influence that the Red Power movement brought to national Indian policy and the awareness of Indian concerns. Also the revised edition emphasized the importance of independent community-based projects. While the first edition was clearly aimed at a non-Native reader, the second attempted to reach both audiences, and especially a young, politically active, pan-tribal audience. It offered young Indian readers a political and historical understanding of the present struggle and proposed the community as the locus of political activity.

In 1962, McNickle concluded his *Indian Tribes of the United States* with a quotation from the "Declaration of Indian Purpose," which was composed during the 1961 University of Chicago conference where Indian representatives from ninety tribes gathered. For McNickle, this event marked the advent of an era of pan-tribalism even more than did the creation of the National Congress of American Indians in 1944. The manifesto, aimed at non-Native America, pleads for material assistance but also asks for ample time to adjust to the pressure from the dominant culture without interference. In 1973, McNickle revised *Indian Tribes of the United States,* changing the title to *Native American Tribalism: Indian Survivals and Renewals.* In this new edition, McNickle added an epilogue that concerned the Alaska Native Claims Settlement Act; in it he expressed the opinion that the act was a victory for Indians because the government had been forced to accept a proposal that would assure some measure of Native self-determination (167). The new conclusion emphasized the oscillation of Federal Indian policy, its periodic acceptance and then denial of Native rights. The section ended by expressing cautious hope that a policy of self-determination was about to be universally accepted. McNickle cited the government's return of the Taos Pueblo sacred lake, whose significance was religious rather than economic, as an example of greater tolerance by contemporary America, and he insisted that the efforts of the new Native American writers were vital to the growing sense of pan-tribalism (168). McNickle believed that though the elders might not be comfortable with the terms *pan-tribalism* and *Indian nationalism*, they were sure of their common identity. The angry young people would have to find common ground in their different senses of tribal identity, and they would also need to understand the political necessity of pan-tribal unity. McNickle concluded: "Finally, it can be noted in closing that the spokesmen of earlier years who tried to accept what an alien world offered their people, seeing no other choice open, are now silent. If the Indian race is to be destroyed, the new voices avow, the destroying agent will have to contend with an integrating people, not with isolated individuals lost in anonymity" (170). Thus, in this concluding chapter when discussing the relations between elders and politically active youth, McNickle clearly emphasizes the role of pan-tribal rather than tribal-specific identity. When he reminded the youth of the vascillation of white attitudes toward Natives, he also advised them to use those attitudes, when encountered, to further the cause of Native rights, but not to be lulled into a false sense of security. *Wind from an Enemy Sky* reinforces and dramatizes this advice.

In his introduction to *Native American Tribalism*, McNickle included a section pointedly aimed at militant youth. He criticized AIM's attempt to use the BIA to dissolve the Sioux IRA constitution, claiming that if this were to have happened, "the last vestige of a tribe's sovereign right to govern itself in internal matters would have vanished" (xi). These questions of identity, relations to elders, political strategy, and the dynamics of American perception of Indians, map the field of Indian political discourse to which McNickle saw himself responding. His experience of working with Indian youth, university students, and scholarship committees, and as a lecturer and reviewer kept him abreast of current Indian affairs and mindful that there was a young Native audience out there for him.

Wind from an Enemy Sky addresses this pan-tribal and political young audience in some very specific ways and for some very specific goals. One way it does this is through reference to specific events that McNickle actually experienced. The BIA reform administration that in the novel places the educated social worker in the Little Elk agency is obviously modeled after the Collier administration. The dam on Little Elk land in the novel was probably not modeled after Kerr Dam. The Flathead tribe was relatively receptive to that dam (Dunsmore 40). More likely, the dam in *Wind* was inspired by Garrison dam near Fort Berthold. Controversy surrounded the construction of this dam because it flooded sacred burial sites. The South American dam of the novel paralleled a real South American dam project with which he was familiar. Likewise, much of the action in *Wind* centers on the Indians' attempt to have the Feather Boy sacred bundle returned. McNickle worked on the successful negotiations to return the Mandan sacred bundle,[3] but the most recent event in his mind might have been the successful return of the sacred lake to Taos Pueblo. In both cases, the tribes were successful in having sacred objects returned.

Clearly the landscape in the novel resembles the geography of the Salish reservation where McNickle grew up. Similarly, some of the characters in the novel resemble real life figures. McNickle's diaries for 1957 discussed the quarrel between two brothers in Crownpoint, New Mexico. The quarrel was very political and involved issues concerning leadership of some local organizations. The tensions were high because one brother was considered educated and one not. Significantly, the uneducated brother was named Sam Jim.

It would appear that McNickle adapted some historical and political events for his literary goals. I think this kind of adaptation, which Iser refers to as *depragmatization*, is the source of much of McNickle's creative structuring in *Wind*. Iser explains the general process:

> A further complication consists in the fact that literary texts do not serve merely to denote empirically existing objects. Even though they may select objects from the empirical world . . . they depragmatize them, for these objects are not to be denoted. The literary text, however, takes its selected objects out of their pragmatic context and so shatters their original frame of reference; the result is to reveal aspects (e.g. of social norms) which had remained hidden as long as the frame of reference remained intact. (109)

The incorporation of known political events required for McNickle a depragmatization unlike that in Welch's *Winter in the Blood* or in Erdrich's *Love Medicine*. The events in these two novels are not of such a political nature that their denotations must be completely depragmatized. In *Wind*, the denotations of events are not only depragmatized but transformed because the frame of reference is so strongly fixed in the perspective of both audiences. In pushing for a pan-tribal frame of reference, McNickle engaged a highly political discourse about progress and violence in Native communities. The discourse was drawn from the political conversations of educated Indian youth conducted in publications like *Akwesasne Notes* during the mid-seventies.[4] He depragmatized the dam project, the successfully returned bundle, and the victory of the Taos Pueblo in order to "heighten the contradictions" (as activists from the seventies phrased it) inherent in Native/non-Native relations.

He went on to identify in the conclusion to *Native American Tribalism* the vital role Indian artists and intellectuals played in expressing tribal views, in voicing common goals, and in identifying similar problems. He saw their contribution as essential in establishing a basis for the pan-Indian perspective. Soon after writing this conclusion, he moved on to completing his final revision of *Wind*. In writing his text, he attempted to play the same role he assigned to other Native writers: that of fostering a pan-tribal perspective in his Native readers.

In *Wind*, McNickle's implied Native reader is expected to recognize that cultural unity is more important than any issue facing an Indian group. Henry Jim's lesson is that only if the people are united will significant change come about and that change can only proceed at the pace set by the people themselves. The struggle between Henry Jim and Bull forces the implied Native reader to adopt an opinion on the traditionalist/progressive debate that is the subtext of the novel. The necessity of cultural unity on the textual level is mirrored by the necessity of unity on the national political level. The activist cannot separate himself from the people and set himself up as a model on the communal or national arena. The alien concept of individual responsibility would not only deconstruct that person's Indian identity, but it would impede the social dynamic necessary for change. Only if the forces of a unified society confronted the forces of the status-quo could positive change come about. In a letter to Sol Tax, McNickle explained:

> I think you are quite right, i.e., perceptive, in your observation that what most disrupts tribal capacity to act, (to carry on), is the divisiveness that results from imposing an alien concept of individual responsibility in the group. The pulling and hauling between (traditionalist) and (progressive) parties which characterizes so many Indian communities flows immediately from this outside imposition. Every Indian generation has to be made over in the quest for harmony. Fortunately, it always seems to work out and the community in the end remains intact; but at great cost. And to add to the travail, the Indians are blamed for their factional splits, as if they were in charge and able to prevent self-injury. The answer, as you rightly assume, is to restore the autonomy they once enjoyed, which made possible useful and meaningful adaptations.[5]

The ultimate effects of federal policy or tribal decisions on tribal communities may not be clearly visible. Indeed, controlling the outcome of such restructuring may be out of the hands of tribal communities, but the internal social dynamic and especially the creation of identity *are* open to structuring. McNickle believed that each Indian generation remade itself: personally, culturally, and, in the contemporary world, politically. *Wind from an Enemy Sky* emerged out of a field of tumultuous discourse on identity, community, and political action.

What did you see? What did you learn? These two questions condense the responses of both sets of implied readers as the text becomes a self-conscious attempt to engage both recent and long-standing cultural conversations, to respond to positions, ideas, actions, fears, and events: to define identity by speaking.

The remaking of a new Indian generation is not accomplished in *Wind*. It remains a task to be completed by both implied readers, though it may be a more essential act of survival for the Native reader. McNickle prepares implied readers for such a mediation by establishing and redirecting the cultural conversations in the text. The multiple narratives of identity are separated in a way that they are not in *The Surrounded*. *The Surrounded* explores the identity of a lone male protagonist; *Wind*, however, casts a whole group, the Little Elk Indians, in that role. Their identity as a continuous whole must be carefully constructed from a variety of narrative realities.

The psychological narrative at the center of *Wind* concerns Bull's movement from fear and anger to pride and strength. McNickle implies that pride and strength are necessary for a true sense of identity to emerge; Bull directs his last words toward young Antoine because he hopes that Antoine can learn from his psychological change and use this knowledge to form his own and his people's sense of identity. However, Bull knows it must not be an identity that is defined by anger since anger might "eat out the guts" (131). Antoine will need to overcome the fear that he learned in boarding school (106) by drawing upon the power of a united people. The people too must abandon their isolation and fear. Bull's pride must define the community without directing itself toward violence; however, repressing the pride altogether could also lead to violent results.

Adam Pell is the only other character whose psychological story is developed, but Pell's reformist actions might be more selfish than Bull's since they appear to be motivated by guilt, ego, or a romantic fascination with the exotic. He is a foil to Bull since he is locked in his own psychologically defined identity. His quest to have something to give, "to show good faith" (210), and "to make amends" (215), reveals a Western emphasis on individual action as the source of personal definition. Pell does not change his belief in individualistic action, though he may substitute one set of values for another.

McNickle downplays the psychological story partly because of its inherent emphasis on individualism. Instead, he foregrounds the sociological and cultural stories of identity, especially in his portrayal of Henry Jim. Jim rejects his culturally defined identity as a chief and to a certain extent as an Indian. He wishes to lead the people to new ways and break the hold of the past. He becomes the white man's showpiece, farming in the valley and living in a white man's house. He assumes the Western social role of a leader who is a model, whose individual actions set a standard for others to follow. However, the people do not follow him. This sociological identity holds until Jim approaches death. Then he resumes his cultural identity as indicated by his trip to the mountain, his desire to retrieve the Feather Boy medicine bundle, his speaking the Little Elk language, and his move into a tepee. When he does all this he reestablishes his identity as a chief, for a chief is not a model individual separated from his group but "is expected to take care of the people. When someone is hungry, he shares what he has. He steps in between when they are quarreling" (21). At the end, Jim reinvests himself in this role.

A second area of cultural identity is implied by the text. Bull's return to pride marks Antoine's starting point of cultural identity. Though marred by the violence of Native/non-Native encounters, Antoine and the people are ready to develop as a unified whole, if only the government will give them time and the room to maneuver. Both Bull (180) and Rafferty (179) note the change.

McNickle backgrounds the mythic identity narrative partly because he does not want to reinforce the romantic stereotypes reinvigorated in the counterculture of the 1960s. McNickle did not want his non-Native audience to conclude that Indian mysticism was the path to cross-cultural understanding. Yet his task in *Wind* is to demonstrate that it is a traditional, significant, and legitimate epistemological mode. As a way of thinking, learning and experiencing, it has shaped Native thought. He does not strive to have either implied reader experience the mythic narrative as Silko and Vizenor do, but rather he encourages non-Native readers to know it is there and that it is legitimate. While not participating in a mythic narrative, Native readers will be reminded of the source of much traditional wisdom.

In essence, McNickle is repragmatizing the mythic level of reality, saying that it is a way of knowing that often reveals the same truth as do other modes of perception. For instance, when Louis challenges Two Sleeps about his foreknowledge of Henry Jim's visit, Two Sleeps replies: "How did I know, bitter mouth? by listening to my grandfather, the badger. And to my Aunt, the bluebird. When a light flickers, when a star falls, we know death will come for somebody. And we saw the lantern move tonight. But I have a simpler answer. People have been coming to me to tell me that the man was traveling everywhere and would come here to make peace with this camp. That is how I know, bitter mouth." (20) Thus two modes of perception lead Two Sleeps to similar knowledge. Later in the novel, he learns of the loss of Feather Boy and the tragedy at the end before the readers do, but the reader's observation and analysis lead to the same knowledge. Two Sleeps does not reveal the bad news because he fears creating hard feelings, but more deeply because he knows both the loss of Feather Boy and the loss of Bull are preordained. There is nothing he can do about it. Vision must be accompanied by action.

Consequently, the Feather Boy bundle is repragmatized as the symbol of lost unity and of the past as opposed to representing some mystical transcendent source of wisdom. The myth/story told about the bundle is that Feather Boy has placed all good things in it to keep the people strong in their world. Even though the people were mean and cared only about food, Feather Boy brought them tobacco so that they could pray. In this way, the material is recognized as subservient to the spiritual. However, the spiritual is a realm of perception accessible through the natural world, as Two Sleeps informs us when he speaks of dreams: "To be born was not enough. To live in the world was not enough. . . . One had to reach. . . . He had to reach with his mind into all things, the things that grew from small beginnings and the things that stayed firmly placed and enduring. He had to know more and more, until he himself dissolved and became part of everything else—and then he would know certainly. . . . That was something of what it was like to be in the world" (198).

Two Sleeps and Antoine are the only characters who the reader knows experience this level of perception. Both are tied to the earth power in the land around them. While both implied Native and non-Native readers are positioned so that they follow Two Sleeps's unifying experience, the novel focuses on the pragmatic results of that vision more than the experiencing of the process. And while becoming "part of everything" allows humankind to bond to the world around it, the implication seems to be that the world has changed or that it "fell apart" (256), and that a new vision, a new certainty, will need to be mediated. The identity of the Little Elk Indians as a specific historical formulation, or as McNickle might say, the fit of an individual to the world, is forever broken when the Feather Boy bundle is lost. The elements of identity posited in Bull, Henry Jim, and Two Sleeps must be united and reconfigured in Antoine, for out of him will emerge a renewed Indian identity.

Celebrating Culture

Love Medicine

◆

> Contemporary Native American Writers have therefore a task
> quite different from that of other writers I've mentioned. In
> light of enormous loss, they must tell the stories of contempo-
> rary survivors while protecting and celebrating the cores of
> cultures left in the wake of catastrophe.
> —Louise Erdrich,
> "Where I Ought to Be"

*L*ove Medicine is a dazzling, personal, intense novel of survivors, who struggle to define their own identities and fates
in a world of mystery and human frailty. In her writing,
Louise Erdrich attempts both to protect and celebrate this
world. To effectively assume the roles of protector and cele-
brant, Erdrich must mediate between two conceptual frameworks, non-Native and Native, in order to avoid future catastrophes. She endeavors to manipulate each audience so that it
will experience the novel through the paths of understanding
unique to each culture, thus assuring protection and continuance of a newly appreciated and experienced Native American epistemological reality.

Celebrating and protecting the stories of survivors of cross-cultural catastrophe can imply the creation of characters formed by competing senses of identity. Many people have commented that cultural concepts of identity appear to differ in Native American and non-Native cultures. For example, Lincoln refers to Native Americans' "alternative senses of family, kinship, communal property, lineage, language, history, geography, even space-time conceptions." ("Indi'n" 216). For both Native and non-Native implied readers, the stories Erdrich tells address, clarify, and define the various ways that identity exists in both cultural frameworks. As she layers these identities in the text, they become visible through the merging of epistemological codes that are used to signify psychological, social, communal, and mythic senses of identity. The mediational actions of the author serve to protect and celebrate culture by a continuing recreation of the multiple facets of identity through multiple narratives allowing negotiation to replace simple concepts of identity in either system.

Mediation, as the generative organizational principle, often downplays mechanically plotted novel structures while encouraging multiple narratives. In this process the voices and ideas of a variety of culturally linked positions, a variety of identities, compete for the reader's ear and thus his or her allegiance. They also engage both Native and non-Native discourse fields. This "struggle going on within discourse," as Bakhtin calls it, characterizes many mediational texts whose nature is essentially dialogic. For Erdrich, plot is far less important than the voices of her characters. She posits the tribal language against the half-breed language and the contemporary American language, evoking discourse fields only to realign their original speaker positions. Bakhtin, in his discussion of narrative discourse, offered an insight useful to understanding the relationship of plot to language in Erdrich's work. He wrote of plot serving to "represent speaking persons and their ideological worlds." In the process of reading a novel, the reader is compelled by dialogics (and doubly so, by mediation) to come "to know one's own language" and "one's own belief system in someone else's system." This process, as I have noted before, is referred to by Bakhtin as "ideological translation" (*Dialogic* 365). *Love Medicine* is a successful mediational novel because the plot organizes the different social languages and ideologies in such a way as to allow the reader into a new way of seeing and speaking about the world, thus promoting ideological translation. For Erdrich, this new perspective for the implied reader is a dynamic one where he or she can adopt a variety of perspectives from the Native and non-Native cultural spectrum. *Love Medicine* then becomes for the reader what Bakhtin envisions: "the experience of a discourse, a world view, and an ideologically based act . . . " (365). Erdrich's goals include nothing less than ideological and epistemological transposition since the implied non-Native reader is exposed to Native values and the implied Native reader is shown that new perspectives and new languages can sustain cores of culture.

To understand Erdrich's mediational positioning, we can consider the discourses embedded in the text. She attempts to present an oral discourse in a written format. Erdrich's first person narrators talk directly to both implied readers as if they were chatting around a kitchen table. They speculate, remember, complain, come to conclusions, and describe their actions; indeed, almost all the information, the meaning, the significance of the novel is developed through this homage to the most personal and least codified type of oral communication. Private, personal narratives, the most informal of all oral communication, carry the feel of gossip and confession. Scott Sanders has likened reading *Love Medicine* to "being drawn into a boisterous family reunion in a crowded kitchen" (7). Oral tradition in this book defines the nature of all knowledge; for characters like Lipsha what they hear defines who they are.

Each character's personal narration competes with another's, and whatever significance is developed, is created by the constant interplay of events and their interpretation. Kay Sands suggests the importance of these personal oral narratives when she writes, "The source of her [Erdrich's] storytelling technique is the secular anecdotal narrative process of community gossip, the storytelling sanction toward proper behavior that works so effectively in Indian communities to identify membership in the group and insure survival of group values and its valued individuals. . . . Gossip affirms identity, provides information, and binds the absent to the family and the community" ("Review" 14).

Yet Erdrich's effort is structured by a set of highly Western novelistic conventions that have contemporary parallels in experimental novels, semiotic poetry, and cinéma vérité. Catherine Rainwater suggests that Erdrich's novels engage the familiar discourse of "Western family saga" only to redirect it (418). Erdrich never seems to be totally content with letting the characters speak solely for themselves. The author makes her presence known both through the voice of a third-person omniscient narrator and in her use of highly structured images that resonate symbolically through each section, especially those that close each section. Robert Silberman posits that Native writers, and especially Erdrich, in their attempts to move writing toward storytelling, have been developing "conventions of the oral," conventions every bit as necessary for generation of the text as the conventions of realism or naturalism (118). He identifies the use of a dramatic present tense and the occasional address to the reader with the second person pronoun, "you." But an examination of oral tradition would quickly add many more elements to the list. Erdrich's constant switching from past to present tense, her shifts from omniscient to first-person narration, her episodic structure, her use of dialect, and her use of foreshadowing and flashbacks, provide an evocative rendition of a traditional storyteller's art.

However, it is also clear that what we have is a novel, a

Western structure, whose task it is to recreate something of a Native oral tradition. Erdrich uses a Western field of discourse to arrive at a Native perspective and illuminates the conventions, significations, assumptions, and strengths of both as she does so. In adopting oral features for her novel, her goal is not to be a traditional storyteller, nor is it merely to add a sense of immediacy to her novel. Rather, her primary purpose is to position both audiences to accept an oral discourse whose codes she can mediate. Through this mediation, she shows both audiences how to value contemporary Native ways of meaning and thereby contemporary Native cultures—the ultimate sources of value in the novel.

Humorous examples of the oral style of Erdrich's mediation in *Love Medicine* are found in Lipsha Morrisey's malapropisms. Lipsha, who has taken some college classes, alternates, as Albertine tells us, between using "words I had to ask him the meaning of," and not making "the simplest sense" (36). Lipsha's malapropisms, such as when he refers to "mental condensation" (199) when he means concentration, or when he says he was in a "laundry" (192) when he means quandary, reveal his lack of familiarity with a vocabulary that is learned from reading rather than conversation.[1] Yet Lipsha can also turn around the use the vocabulary of conversation to create an illuminating metaphor. At a moment when death surrounds him, Lipsha likens his revelations about himself and the world to a video game: "You play those games never knowing what you see. When I fell into the dream alongside both of them [Grandpa and Grandma Kashpaw] I saw that the dominions I had defended myself from anciently was but delusions of the screen. Blips of light. And I was scot-free now, whistling through space" (210). His mediational style of expression reveals Erdrich's concern with embedding every level of epistemological double-code and with engaging a number of discourse fields at once. Lipsha enters traditional religious discourse and, at the same time, employs contemporary Indian humor and the discourse of pop culture.[2]

If one considers the larger goals of this mediational pro-cess, much of the richness of the text emerges. Central to a Chippewa world view, and that of much of Native America, is a sense of the reciprocal nature of the relationships between human beings and the spiritual powers that activate the world. A person's actions in the natural world have spiritual repercussions. For instance, an Eskimo elder, worried about the actions of his people and the response of the spirit world, once said, "No bears have come because there is no ice, and there is no ice because there is no wind, and there is no wind because we have offended the powers" (qtd. in Alfonso Ortiz 18). The reciprocal relationship between human beings and nature, and human beings and the spirit world, is also portrayed in *Love Medicine*. In the novel, the survival of individuals is the function of a reciprocal relationship that they establish with the spiritual powers of the universe. The touch that Lipsha loses and regains, or Gordie's relationship with June, are examples of negotiations for survival with the universe in which they participate. Erdrich seems to be assuming the complete interpenetration of the tangible and intangible worlds. Much Native American thought assumes that mental and physical phenomena are inseparable, and that thought and speech can deeply influence a natural world where no circumstance is accidental or free from person-alized intent. As Allen writes:

> It is reasonable that all literary forms should be interrelated, given the basic idea of the unity and relatedness of all the phenomena of life. Separation of parts into this or that catego-ry is not agreeable to American Indians, and the attempt to separate essentially unified phenomena results in distortion. . . . The purpose of a ceremony is to integrate: to fuse the individual with his or her fellows, the community of people with that of the other kingdoms, and this larger communal group with the worlds beyond this one. (*Sacred* 62)

With their emphasis on ceremony, Native Americans unify the various levels of meaning that Western non-Natives tend to separate. This unity of experience is what Joseph Epes Brown refers to as "a polysynthetic metaphysic of nature" (30).[3] Erdrich merges this Native sense of multiple levels of meaning for each physical act with a powerful belief in the mystery of events. What begins on a physical level may start to take on a larger significance, but Erdrich leaves the connections mysterious. These mysterious connections show both the characters and the implied readers the paths to sacred processes of the universe. For example, Nector takes Marie on a path during what appears to be a moment of heedless lust, but both are caught up in an event that defines their lives. They give themselves over to a mysterious force that shapes their spirits. Only years later do they understand something of that mystery. Understanding slowly builds in the novel as people tell us more of their stories. Events, which in Western thought would have only physical significance, take on spiritual, mythic, cultural, personal, and religious significance. As Rainwater notes, Erdrich's novels "confront the problems of origination of knowledge . . . " (413). In them, the implied non-Native reader is coaxed "to abandon fixed notions about what kinds of experience are 'important'" (416). New possibilities are now credible. Reciprocity between the various levels of existence ties the meaning together and helps Erdrich express a Chippewa world view that appreciates a dynamic process of signification, or as Allen so strikingly puts it, a world view that sees the "self as a moving event within a moving universe," a universe where "everything moves in dynamic equilibrium" (*Sacred* 147). By encoding this alternate way of creating meaning, Erdrich challenges the implied non-Native reader.

On the other hand, Erdrich has an alternative goal: to present a complementary vision of individual will and history that is more psychologically based than communally oriented. The effects of Nector's actions on those around him, the exploration of Marie in terms of her relationship to the nun, Sister Leopolda, and King's vision of his life, all suggest a psychological dimension that uses dominant culture conceptual categories. Moreover, the novel clearly displays a sociological agenda as illustrated by its treatment of such themes as changes in family structure and the influences on the reservation of the dominant society, especially its Christian segment. The implied Native reader is encouraged to perceive levels of text such as these in terms of Western analysis.

This use of both cognitive systems to illuminate each other supports Bakhtin's understanding of the novel's task: a "coming to know one's own belief system in someone else's system." As Hayden White has pointed out, this is a self-reflexive act, one where the reader's personal involvement is demanded in the process of reading and misreading the text. In creating meaning, both implied readers will reevaluate their own system and each other's. This process is integral to Erdrich's goals as a "citizen of two nations" ("A Conversation"). Sands observes: "There is a sort of double-think demanded by Erdrich. The incidents must be carried in the reader's mind, constantly reshuffled and reinterpreted as new events are revealed and the narrative biases of each character are exposed" ("Review" 18).[4] Rainwater sees the text as maneuvering the reader into a position "between Worlds," which frustrates one's expectations of Western narrativity: "This frustration amounts to a textually induced or encoded experience of marginality as the foremost component of the reader's response" (406). From this position, the reader will be required to "consider perceptual frameworks as important structural principles in both textual and nontextual realms" (412). Ultimately the reader's new perceptual position allows him or her to consider the possibility that "the world takes on the shapes of the stories we tell" (422). Both Rainwater and Sands emphasize the deep level restructuring required of the implied non-Native reader.[5]

One example of how these two perceptual frameworks merge in the text lies in the portrayal of Henry Lamartine.

According to a Western set of epistemological codes, he is clearly a prototype of the displaced soldier returning home; the reader can easily respond to his situation with the commonplace insight that the experience of combat often destroys the soldier's sense of reality, making it difficult if not impossible to reintegrate himself back into society. We know this by looking at the chronological series of events in his life, drawing a set of inferences based on causal reasoning. When he dies, we are not surprised since we have drawn a straight line from the shattering experience early in his life to his inevitable death. We have seen many stories like this; the ending is a convention of stories of returned veterans. However, Henry's story seems more socially complex when both implied readers also consider that his war was the Vietnam war with all its political controversy and high number of minority participants. With these non-Native social and psychological codes giving meaning to the events of Henry's life, the implied non-Native reader has an easy-to-read, satisfying text, complete with closure. When Lyman drives the red convertible into the river after Henry has drowned, the psychological orientation of the implied non-Native reader encourages the conclusions that Henry committed suicide and that Lyman wished to make the suicide look like an accident in order to save his brother's reputation.

However, a Native perspective leads to a different interpretation of events. Henry's inability to resume normal life at home and his subsequent death can be seen as resulting from the fact that his actions are out of harmony with the Chippewa sense of war, death, honor, and right thinking. As a draftee, Henry has no choice in his actions. He does not go off to war with a vision that will give him power, nor does he dance the warrior's dance. He has not participated in any ritual actions that will let the souls of his dead enemies rest.[6] In the one wartime action of Henry's we learn about, he is ordered to interrogate a dying woman who claims the bond of relationship with him. His implication in the death of a relative puts him in conflict with Chippewa cultural values. He is not prepared ritually for his departure for war, he breaks the bonds of kinship, and, because his mother is afraid to take him to the old medicine man, he is not purified of the spirits of dead enemies when he returns. At the end of the chapter entitled "The Red Convertible," Henry's renewal of interest in his brother and in the wild dance seem to undercut the possibility of psychologically motivated suicide. His one comment as he stands in the water, "My boots are filling up," does not have the purposeful ring of someone who is committing suicide. Perhaps his drowning, which is performed in an unpurified state, can be understood as a response to Henry's improper behavior by the spiritual forces of the world around us—the water spirits' revenge.[7] As the balance is set right again, Lyman's driving of the car into the river represents the custom of burying the dead person's private possessions along with him.

Each of these two perspectives on the meaning of the character Henry has a certain level of completeness, yet the novel's richness is revealed when each story, each narrative viewpoint, is seen in contrast to the other. Since each perspective creates a coherent and meaningful story, implied readers are given a chance to experience complementary meaning structures. Yet their differences encourage a self-reflexive examination of familiar patterns of thought as the legitimacy of other forms becomes clear.

The psychological interpretation underlies and enriches the cultural one. As Michael Dorris has remarked, he and Erdrich are always concerned with giving "the readers a choice" between a "mystical reason" and "a more psychological explanation" ("A Conversation"). Both stories' realities present valid world views and can stand alone to explain the meaning of the actions, yet each level of the text forces us to question exactly what we as readers believe. Can both be right? Can one be righ and the other wrong? It seems clear that each reveals the strengths and weaknesses of the other code. An understanding of each level enhances our understanding of the other. The use of one cultural code to illuminate the other is best shown in Erdrich's treatment of ghosts in *Love Medicine*. While ghosts are a very real part of the Chippewa world view, they are not believed to be often troubling to the living if dealt with properly. Landes observes that it still was a time of great danger, where careful action was required of the people: "The passage from life was considered tricky, beset with personified evils intent on murdering the wandering soul" ("Ojibway Religion" 87–88). But the proper instructions and recommendations delivered over a grave would assure the soul passage to the village of shadows. Conventional Western thought does not consider ghosts as real. While we allow them entrance into our world through literature, especially children's tales, ghosts are generally considered to be a storytelling convention with no substance. So when Gordie sees June's ghost, a reader whose orientations are Western will not see the encounter as real but will instead see it as a delusion brought on by alcohol and grief. That in his drunken frenzy Gordie should hit a deer and mistake it for June has no meaning other than as a revelation of his psychological state of mind; it does not seem surprising that at the end of the encounter with Sister Mary Martin, he should end up running mad in the woods. However, in the traditional Chippewa world view, the spirit world is the source of special insight and power. Human and non-human beings can be transformed to assume a variety of appearances. A. Irving Hallowell, in discussing Ojibwa world view, notes: "Both living and dead human beings may assume the form of animals. So far as appearance is concerned, there is no hard and fast line that can be drawn between animal form and human form because metamorphosis is possible" (38).

According to traditional Chippewa custom, a dead wife returning to visit the husband who abused her would not be surprising, especially if she has not been buried in the appropriate manner. At the time of her death, June was unable to complete her journey home. Her ghostly visit to Gordie completes her return but also allows her wandering spirit to find the path to the spirit world. She visits Gordie because he has called her name and thus violated one of the most important prohibitions designed to keep the spirits of the dead on the trail to the spirit world. It is understandable that June would use a deer to aid her visit, as the spirits of animals are much closer to the world of the spirit than humans are, and the cultural perception of the deer as a willing prey adds ironic resonance. When Gordie clubs the deer with the tire iron, it is an action reminiscent of the times he hit his wife when she was alive. Therefore his confession to the nun that he has killed June carries a ring of ironic truth and becomes more than the baseless ravings of a crazed drunk; he provides for implied Native readers insight how into actions can take place on an other-than-human plane. Indeed, Barnouw, in his discussion of Chippewa oral narratives, observes the importance of "the notion that visible forms are deceptive and that human and animal forms are interchangeable" (247).[8] Such a Chippewa epistemological position clearly informs many of the events in the text.

The return of Nector Kashpaw's ghost also expresses the text's mediational positioning. The suddenness of Nector's death deprives him of the chance to say good-bye to the two women he loves. Lipsha and Marie observe that when ghosts return they have a "certain uneasy reason to come back" (212). He visits Lulu, Lipsha, and Marie until he is persuaded to go back to the spirit world of Lipsha, who has accidentally killed him. Nector's visit cannot be explained away, as in the case of Gordie, as a drunken hallucination. Psychologically we can explain the presence of the ghost as being a figment of the women's imagination under the stress of grief. However, even by Western epistemological standards, three independent visits observed by three independent observers come dangerously close to constituting corroborated reality. However, the reality they tend to corroborate is one in which Western tradition places no credence. Yet in Chippewa religious thought, the concept of a return to life is central. Barnouw notes that this concept is "implicit in the Midewiwin ceremony, in which members shoot one another with their medicine hides but come back to life again" (252). Lipsha comments on the puzzling interaction of the human and spirit worlds: "Whether or not he had been there is not the point. She had *seen* him, and that meant anyone else could see him, too. Not only that but, as is usually the case with these here ghosts, he had a certain uneasy reason to come back. And of course Grandma Kashpaw had scanned it out" (212).

Lipsha's comments convey both readers' attitudes toward the reality of ghosts and thus validate each world view and epistemological framework. On the one hand, he seems to say that it might not matter if the ghost was real since it was real to Grandma in her altered psychological state. On the other hand, Lipsha also says that if she saw him, others could see him—a statement that attributes to the ghost an objective reality. When he refers to the ghost's motivation in coming back, he shows that his own belief in the existence of the spirit world and of ghosts is undisturbed. There is no question that the ghost was there, because his spirit is still around; the problem is not that he cannot, but rather that he *can* be seen and that he refuses to let go of this world. The ghost needs to be instructed as to what to do, and Lipsha's admonition to Nector's ghost to return to the company of the spirits parallels recorded Midewiwin orations to the dead.

The thrust of such mediational discourse is to take a Western issue of non-truth—or non-reality—and treat it with the assumptions of Chippewa reality while layering psychological motivation and Native custom. Each code is used and illuminates the other. The end result of Erdrich's technique is that both implied readers are forced to look at the multiple meanings of an event. And both implied readers must hold all these versions of reality together in some meaningful mediational structure. Sands points out: "It is, of course, the very method of the novel, individuals telling individual stories, that not only creates the multiple effect of the novel but requires a mediator, the reader, to bring the episodes together" ("Review" 20). These implied readers must follow the text so as to mediate between stories, cultural codes, definitions of identity, and versions of reality.

Clearly the two sets of cultural codes produce a doubling of narrative textures as distinct as the two implied readers Erdrich tries to reach. Each implied reader is satisfied in many ways but primarily by the developing sense of identity as they animate the emerging characters. The contemporary survivors that Erdrich depicts are people for whom navigating change and defining identity are vitally important ways to protect and celebrate individual and cultural values. Since both audiences experience the variety of culturally framed definitions of identity, part of the ideological translation of which Bakhtin wrote is accomplished. Both implied readers must actively work to read the narratives in a unified manner, never completely sure they are reading it right or reading it completely. This active, self-reflexive role of the implied readers in Erdrich's mediation is required when they begin to understand the multiple narratives through which she achieves "ideological translation." Sands observes: "The novel places the reader simultaneously on the fringe of the story yet at the very center of the process—distant and intimate, passive yet very actively involved in the narrative process" (12). An implied reader can feel distant from one story reality while intimate with another, appreciating an identity for a character while experiencing a new sense of identity in a different narrative for that same character. Rainwater explains that while Erdrich's texts suggest traditional Western definitions of identity, they "are also traversed by a conflicting code which has to do with American Indian concepts of individuation that are not based on psychological essence or individual psychology" (421).[9]

Returning to Henry Lamartine for a moment will clarify the functioning of multiple narrative in *Love Medicine*. How does a reader define Henry's identity? Surely his identity can be defined sociologically when he is seen as a shell-shocked veteran unable to adjust to the world back home, but as I have suggested, he can also be seen as a warrior haunted by the ghosts of his dead enemies that he cannot ritualistically expel. Through this latter perspective, Henry is given a communal role, an identity based on his relation to the community and family as a young warrior and dutiful son. Each sense of identity satisfies its appropriate audience, but also because both implied readers hold at once two senses of identity, the text validates both perspectives. Even more central to the novel are the stories that define Nector's identity. Nector comes from a family that is "respected as the last hereditary leaders of this tribe" (89). His communal identity is set from the beginning and much of his life is an attempt to live up to that identity, to understand it and grow into it. The Kashpaw sense of worth and the Chippewa tradition constitute the essence of how Nector sees himself. Socially, he is the tribal chairman. While the dominant culture would assume that this status places him as the leader of his tribe, tribal custom does not give him that role unless he can live up to the traditional function of the leader. Nector's psychological sense of identity as someone with no control over events, however, undermines this Western social definition as leader in much the same way his communal role as a Kashpaw supports it. He is both a communal leader and a follower because, as he says, "Chippewa politics was thorns in my jeans" (102).

Psychologically, Nector sees himself as floating down a river that has calm spots, rapids, and unexpected branchings. His sense of himself is that of a person being carried along by events as he struggles to maintain control of them. Nector's retreat to apparent senility becomes a way that he can finally completely define himself in the midst of the river flow of emotions and the demands of politics. Lulu recognizes the essential psychological truth of who he is when he says, "People said Nector Kashpaw had changed, but the truth was he'd just become more like himself than ever" (230). Various layers of his identity created by the narrative are embedded in the text and held simultaneously in dialogic interaction by both implied readers.

Marie Lazarre has an identity defined by the community as one of those "dirty Lazarres." Despite her attempts to re-create this identity, the community has defined her role and position in its complex structure. This communal identity is contrasted to her psychological identity as molder of Nector, as defeater of Sister Leopolda, as woman defined by her household. These two senses of identity complement each other. Though she contends to herself "I was solid class" (113), the sociological level remains mostly latent. As wife of the tribal chairman, her social position should be one of leadership, but her communal identity as "a dirty Lazarre" deprives her of this status. As a wife who is left at home during an ongoing extra-marital relationship, her sense of a sociological identity is also undercut. While as a woman who takes in lost children, she performs a social function that helps her clarify her sense of self on the psychological and communal level, she is unable to allow this to help her develop a clearly defined social identity.

Lulu Lamartine plays the communal role of the libertine. As a woman with eight boys and one girl who are fathered by a variety of husbands, she is hated by the wives in the community and loved by their husbands. Though a disrupter of families, her own family is vitally important to her. Her identity as libertine is in contrast to her psychological identity as consummate lover of beauty. After a grisly look at death in her early childhood, she comes to define herself as someone "in love with the whole world and all that lived in its rainy arms" (216). What is viewed from the communal realm as irresponsible action, is for Lulu an honest attempt to drink in beauty and let it fill her up if only for a moment. Each sense of identity enriches the reader's understanding of the other and encourages the audiences to clarify their codes.

While in the other characters discussed, Erdrich has developed something of the psychological, social, and communal stories, in her portrayal of Gerry Nanapush, she displays all four levels of narrative identity. On a sociological level he is the convict Indian turned political hero. As a member of the American Indian movement, he is seen and sees himself as a social symbol to both the non-Native and the Native world, but one who believes in justice, not laws. On a psychological level he is presented as a loving husband and father; as such, Gerry is motivated by personal passions. His communal identity hinges on relationships as son of Old Man Pillager and Lulu Lamartine, lover of June Morrissey, and father to Lipsha Morrissey. As warrior against the social institutions of modern America, Gerry presents the community with an image through which it can project itself as successful and yet evasive, the image of an unwilling warrior who is not destroyed by the spirit of dead enemies, however all-pervasive and overpowering they may be. Yet on a more timeless plane, his actions recall the daring and rebellion of the trickster Nanabosho of Chippewa oral tradition. His magical escapes enhance Chippewa cultural identity while they add to his own idea of himself. Gerry consciously takes on a mythic role and becomes a living embodiment of the trickster.

Lipsha's character is the most obvious expression of the four kinds of narrative identity. Sociologically he is the outcast orphan with no clear parentage. He cares for the aged Nector and Marie out of gratitude but also out of lethargy. His role as orphan and care provider involves a series of social relations that define him but against which he struggles. Psychologically his desire is to find for himself a place in the family that coincides with the unique individual he senses that he is. He sees himself as needing to stay innocent and simple, but he also wants to know about his roots and his background. As Lulu says, "Well, I never thought you was odd. . . . Just troubled. You never knew who you were . . . " (244–45).

Communally Lipsha is a healer, grandson of the powerful old shaman, Old Man Pillager. While his "touch" has been commonly acknowledged on the reservation, his identity as a member of the tribe, with clear family ties and a useful function in the community, has not been acknowledged. After he learns of his true parentage, he confusedly tries to join the Army and become a warrior like his father, Gerry Nanapush. However, it is not on the battlefields of the U.S. Army that he will fight,but on the battlefields of culture and community. By the end of the novel, he learns that he is defined by his family and communal position: "Now as you know, as I have told you, I am sometimes blessed with the talent to touch the sick and heal their individual problems without ever knowing what they are. I have some powers which, now that I think of it, was likely come down from Old Man Pillager. And then there is the newfound fact of insight I inherited from Lulu, as well as the familiar teachings of Grandma Kashpaw on visioning what comes to pass within a lump of tinfoil" (248). With his new realizations come a new understanding of communal identity.

Ultimately, however, Lipsha emerges as the son of trickster Gerry. His mythic identity is linked to the tradition of the powerful trickster/transformer whose job it is to create the form of the world, to modify its contours in keeping with the Earthmaker's plans. Lipsha's medicine trick with the turkey hearts, in keeping with the nature of a trickster's actions, proves to be an event that backfires on him. But this is an event that also is in keeping with the Earthmaker's plan for all beings. Lincoln identifies a Western mythic analogue for Lipsha: "His is the ancient story of the orphan adopted and finally reclaimed by true royalty (June and Gerry as queen and king tricksters). In a comic way, Lipsha figures as the 'divine child' of ancient myth" ("Indi'n" 230). By engaging both Native and non-Native mythic discourse, Erdrich directs the reader's attention to the importance of mythic identity, a decidedly Native epistemological perspective.

Finally, by driving Gerry to freedom, Lipsha concludes a mythic narrative that will live forever in Chippewa imagination. At the bridge, Lipsha physically delivers the trickster Gerry Nanapush[10] to Canada, but this act also takes on communal significance when it is remembered that for many Midewiwin initiates the land of the dead is also called Nehnehbush's land and that the passage from the physical world to the spirit world is made over a bridge (Landes, *Ojibway Religion* 193–99). After Lipsha delivers Gerry to the world of myth, he takes June's wandering soul in hand and prepares to lead her, as he did Nector, to her proper resting place. These actions show us that his identity will be both defined communally as something akin to a Midewiwin official, a healer, and mythically as a new reincarnation of Nehnehbush.

Lipsha concludes that "belonging is a matter of deciding to" (255). This existential realization unifies who he is on the psychological, sociological, communal, and mythic levels; Lipsha thus becomes a complete human being—an experienced adult, a loving son, a healer, and a trickster/transformer. He feels all the threads of identity intertwining and forming a pattern: "In that night I felt expansion, as if the world was branching out in shoots and growing faster than the eye could see. I felt smallness, how the earth divided into bits and kept dividing. I felt stars. I felt them roosting on my shoulders with his hands" (271). Feeling Nanapush's touch still on his shoulder, Lipsha is transformed in a moment of splendid mythic vision. Because he is a new complete human, he thinks of June Morrissey and is strong enough to bring her home, to help her, to help all of the characters in the novel, and to help himself, complete a journey started long ago.

By guiding the reader into experiencing this cosmic unifying vision, Erdrich achieves the ultimate goal of most contemporary Native American literature. As the text embeds the multiple narrative, it compels the implied readers into the same perspective that Lipsha experiences, a perspective from which an individual's perception is expanded and multiple connections are revealed. Lipsha and the other characters of *Love Medicine* embrace the mystery of the world where knowledge, meaning, truth, and signification already exist in a nontangible realm—one that Whorf calls "manifesting." The characters of *Love Medicine* perceive the world as constantly in the process of becoming what it always was; they see meaning in their lives and the world revealing itself, manifesting what has always been there, much in the same way that meaning in Lipsha's life involves the process of letting the forces at work in the world manifest themselves. In *Love Medicine*, Erdrich succeeds in opening the epistemological perspective of the implied non-Native reader to create a more Native American appreciation of meaning and knowledge, one which values the manifesting over the manifested. Implied Native readers, in turn, are positioned to value Western perspectives on meaning.

Erdrich's achievement is to shift the paradigm of both implied readers' thoughts, to recharge implied Native readers and inspire implied non-Native readers with an appreciation of Native American epistemology and world view. As the text opens its mysteries to these readers, perception expands beyond the boundaries of the text, overcoming otherness, and the universe reveals itself as timeless and mythic.

Notes

◆

Introduction

1. Krupat in *Ethnocriticism* challenges Lyotard's postmodernism in terms of its usefulness to ethnic literature and its value in real social discourse.

Chapter 1

1. This use of mediation should be distinguished from Franz Stanzel's use of the term "Mittelbarkeit," usually translated as "mediacy". Stanzel is concerned with a survey of the interaction of person, perspective, and mode as they determine how a narrator mediates between the author and the reader. My analysis seeks to plot the cognitive ground of a specific field of narrative.

2. Ortiz argues this against those who would see contemporary writers as not writing authentic "Indian" literature. For him, the cultural goal overcomes any delegitimatizing influence of the form used: "The ways and methods have been important, but they are important only because of the reason for the struggle. And it is that reason—the struggle against colonialism—which has given substance to what is authentic" ("Toward" 9). Having argued that this struggle engenders a nationalistic quality in contemporary Native American literature, he concludes: "This is the crucial item that has to be understood, that it is entirely possible for a people to retain and maintain their lives through the use of any language. There is not a question of authenticity here; rather it is the way that Indian people have creatively responded to forced colonization" (10). While he tends to see the contemporary Native writer's goal in political terms, I think he

would agree that the realization of the political goal necessitates a restructured cognitive framework for the implied non-Native reader. Such a shift may also be necessary for the implied Native reader who is expected to accept as a cultural tool what was previously seen as a colonial imposition.

3. Iser, following an insight by Booth (137–38), reviews a number of possible terms but settles on *implied reader* as the most useful of them.

4. Genette prefers the term *potential reader.* I adopt *implied reader* because of the wide acceptance of the term.

5. Allen sees much common narrative ground in comtemporary fiction. She writes in "American Indian Fiction, 1968–1983," "For while ritual literature, either of the old-time, traditional variety or the new literary kind, is accretive rather than associative, achronistic rather than synchronistic, and ritual rather than mythological or historical, the new fiction of Europe and America provided a close enough analog to tribal literatures for writers to begin developing a new tribal literary tradition" (1058).

6. See specifically Allen's essay "Where I Come From Is Like This" and "Answering the Deer: Genocide and Continuance in the Poetry of American Indian Women" in her collection *The Sacred Hoop.*

7. Owens, following a similar line of reasoning, intelligently discusses contemporary Native literary texts as hybridized dialogue. Recognizing the Native and non-Native reader implied by the text, he explores heteroglossia and the political situation inherent in the texts (*Other* 11–16).

8. Andrew Wiget explores this "multivocality of some narrative, when the voice of the present narration . . . is located in and made intelligible by its relationship with another, earlier voice also represented in the narration." His analysis seeks to define artistic authority as an effect of this multivocality. However, rather than seeing a dialogic interaction, he interprets identity, voice, and authority as rhetorical constructions "as well as ethnographic reality" ("Identity" 258).

9. See particularly the first three chapters of Wagner's *The Invention of Culture.*

Chapter 2

1. In the Introduction and Epilogue to *American Indian and the Problem of History,* Calvin Martin argues that traditional Native American cultures were characterized by an oral and biological orientation with mythic and timeless connections to the cosmos.

2. Underhill is quoted by Bataille as saying: "Indian narrative style involves a repetition and a dwelling on unimportant detail which confuse the white reader and make it hard for him to follow the story. Motives are never explained and the writer has found even Indians at a loss to interpret them in older myths. Emotional states are summed up in such colorless phrases as 'I like it,' 'I did not like it.' For one deeply immersed in the cultures, the real significance escapes" (89).

3. Sidner Larson contrasts pre-contact "place-oriented notion" of identity with contemporary notions that rest on "self-identification, community

identification, and identification with Native American values" (58–59). It would be a useful study to follow how these elements are arraigned in multiple narratives. See also the definitions by Geary Hobson in his Introduction to *The Remembered Earth,* and Jack D. Forbes, "Determining Who is an Indian."

4. See also Krupat's explorations of Native autobiography as a "synecdochic sense of self" in *Ethnocriticism,* chapter 6, and in "The Dialogic of Silko's *Storyteller.*" Krupat confirms the usefulness of seeking Native American senses of identity as deeply influenced by larger contexts of community and myth, or the I-am-We experience. He even identifies narrative modes such as coup stories and vision narratives that support this orientation.

5. See Eliade, *The Sacred and the Profane: The Nature of Religion.*

Chapter 3

1. Owens observes that Momaday presents "an alienated, deracinated protagonist," who come out of naturalism, "a fragmented cultural context, suffering from a loss of order or structure; a formally experimental, discontinuous narrative replete with multiple perspectivism, stream of consciousness, and so on; and a dependence on mythic structure to provide a way of ordering what T. S. Eliot had called the anarchy and futility of modern existence" (*Other* 91). Similarly, Lincoln in *Native American Renaissance* says about *House Made of Dawn,* "Its prose rhythms, complex narrative points-of-view, flashbacks assimilate experimental techniques in modern fiction and New World romantic themes. Faulkner's interior monologues and multiple time shifts lend a contemporary cast to Lawrence's neoprimitivism" (117). And Strelke observes that what is Western about the novel is the *Angst* of the protagonist, concluding, "The tension between the rural and the industrial/technological is typically a condition of modern western man" (349). Taken together, these assessments define the Western literary discourse that the novel interrogates.

2. Schubnell provides a useful summary of these reviews.

3. Owens tries to establish this oral foundation in his analysis of *House Made of Dawn.* He sees the initial image of Abel running, which is also the final image of the novel, as indicative of Momaday's connection to the storytelling tradition where the audience knows the outcome of the story before the storyteller starts his performance (*Other* 94–95). Yet upon first reading neither implied reader would be familiar enough with the story to know that the image is intended to represent the outcome. Owens seems more convincing when he argues that a Native audience would recognize from oral tradition the "typical pattern of the questing culture hero" (96), but here we might note that such a pattern is universal, as Joseph Campbell suggests. I think the use of this pattern is a mediational element that establishes common ground for both audiences. The idea of the questing culture hero and his emergence journey is also important for Lawrence Evers's analysis of the novel's Native context.

4. Praising what she sees as an effective use of ambiguity, Bernadette Rigal-Cellard provides an extensive discussion of Native and European American elements in the prologue.

5. A great deal has been written about Momaday and the role of imagination. Let me merely reprint the much quoted passage from *Man Made of Words* to show the centrality of imagination to his conception of human existence: "We are what we imagine. Our very existence consists in our imagination. Our best destiny is to imagine, at least, completely, who and what, and that we are" (103). For a more detailed discussion, see Owens, *Other Destinies*, and Schubnell.

6. See also Waniek, Oleson, Nelson, "Snake," and Hogan.

7. Baine Kerr also tries to follow the reader's pattern of reading and misreading to reveal how Momaday has "mythified Indian consciousness into a modern novel" (179).

8. Charles Larson is perhaps the most one-dimensional of these critics since he focuses only on how Momaday presents the relationship between Natives and non-Natives. He excludes any consideration of the themes of continuity and renewal. Seeing Abel's run as a "race toward death, a kind of ritual suicide" (79), Larson decides, "In Momaday's bleak view, the American Indian might just as well beat his head against a wall. The future offers nothing; the past can be recaptured only in fleeting moments. There appears to be little possibility even for simple endurance; the Indian is a vanishing breed" (82). Momaday comments on the dislocation of the psyche in his interview with Coltelli (94). See also Hirsch; Schneider; and Trimmer.

9. While Evers sees this unity as being at the heart of Abel's estrangement, he does not comment on how such an idea of healing might affect the readers (219–29).

10. See Chapter 4, as well as Lincoln, *Indi'n Humor: Bicultural Play in Native America,* for more extended discussions of the importance of Indian humor devices. Momaday himself also notes that he intended to delight the Native reader with a passage where Abel's horse lies down in the river and Abel has to walk out with water squishing out of his shoes (*Ancestral* 32). Perhaps Momaday is referring to the scene in the novel where Abel wears the creaking dead man's shoes (105).

11. Owens also notes: "This is an important message of the novel: evil cannot be destroyed; to attempt to do so is to err seriously and dangerously" (*Other* 104). See also Evers (219–21).

12. Momaday comments on evil in his interview with Charles Woodward: "What is evil? But I would say that it is a negative impulse that motivates us. We go out and deal with evil in various ways. Some of us try to ignore it. Some of us acknowledge it, and some of us confront it. It's a real part of life, I think. . . . I think it [evil] is preexistent. I don't think of it as having an origin that one can point to, anyway. It did not come to be in the Garden of Eden. I think it's there like the concept of the appropriate. Evil is. There is evil in the world, and we are all threatened by it. If you are Ahab, you become obsessed with the idea of confronting it. If you are Billy Budd,

it destroys you" (*Ancestral* 204). In a letter to his publisher, Momaday also refers to the albino as an embodiment of evil in the same manner as is Moby Dick (Schubnell 97, 122). I think the references to Melville do not indicate an influence as much as demonstrate that Momaday intended the novel to focus the Western literary discussion on the struggle between good and evil. Of course, he desired to commandeer that discourse and to move the implied non-Native reader to a perception of the validity and power of a Native view of evil.

13. See Owens (*Other* 103), and Evers (226–27).

14. Suggesting that Momaday's texts are not dialogic, Arnold Krupat writes: "Obviously, Momaday is free to choose whatever stylistic manner he pleases. My intent here is simply to establish that his texts seek to fix that manner univocally; his writing offers a single, invariant poetic voice that everywhere commits itself to subsuming and translating all other voices" (*Voice* 181). While this may be true for *The Names,* I don't think it can be clearly shown for *House Made of Dawn,* considering its multiple voices and the fluid role of its narrator.

15. See Parsons (118–19).

Chapter 4

1. For discussions of alienation, see especially Ruoff, "Alienation," and Sands, "Alienation."

2. Welch provides a summary analysis of the novel when he says: "The winter, I suppose, of *Winter in the Blood* has to do mostly with the character's feeling of distance — as he says, not only from; distance in terms of physical space, but distance in terms of mental space, emotional space. . . . So the problem seems to lie within himself; and I think, probably toward the end, by learning who his grandfather is, by saving the cow, by throwing his grandmother's pouch into her grave, maybe he has lessened that distance somewhat — that emotional distance — which probably would lead to a thawing of that winter in his blood" (Coltelli 191).

3. Larson, in his discussion of American Indian fiction, writes, "With the most recently published novels, however, it is possible to detect the beginnings of a new trend; *Winter in the Blood, Indians' Summer,* and *Ceremony* all appear to be aimed at a reading audience that assumes a higher proportion of Native American readers" (166). Mary Sheldon takes this insight a step further when she tries to identify Welch's, as well as Silko's, goals: "Leslie Marmon Silko and James Welch pose challenges for all readers — Native American, white, hispanic and others. Native American readers are challenged to explore traditional values and beliefs and to live in harmony with the principle truths they hold dear. White readers are challenged to hear within themselves that quiet voice which calls them to respect creation — humanity and plants and animals and stones — and honor it, despite the shrill outcry for more power and possessions dominant in their culture" (124). About this question of Native audiences, Welch states simply, "It's quite large" (Coltelli 196).

4. Kate Vangen describes Indian humor as a tool not only for satire, but also for sociopolitical survival. She deftly outlines the discourse field that *Winter in the Blood* engages. Andrew Horton explores how the ironic humor in the novel becomes a self-protecting mechanism for the narrator. Kenneth Lincoln sees the dark humor as a countervoice to the masking and illusion presented in the novel ("Bad Jokes"). And Alan Velie places Welch's humor in the tradition of the comic novel (*Four*).

5. Allen goes on to argue that because Welch relies on chronological development and causation instead of ritual time, his narrator can never find complete reintegration. In contrast, she sees that Tayo at the end of Silko's *Ceremony* does achieve this reintegration at a point where the narrative has settled into a more conventional structure. Perhaps the distinction between ritual time and chronological time is not easy to perceive in a novel.

6. See Owens, *Other* 128, and Allen, *Sacred* 91–93. Both critics rely on Thackeray.

7. Thackeray's attempt to define for the novel a Gros Ventre discourse field is admirable though other more historical and political approaches might have proved more fruitful. Ruoff goes so far as to suggest that Amos may have become a spirit guide since he appears in the dream that is equated with a vision ("Alienation" 117). That the dream here is not a vision from a vision quest seems apparent. Welch has even agreed that this is not the case (qtd. in Coltelli 187). Suffice it to say that the dream is not the kind of vision that sustains direction, identity, and spiritual connection in either traditional or modern terms. For a helpful discussion of the nature of dreams and visions in Native American culture, I refer the reader to the work of Robin Ridington, especially *Trail to Heaven: Knowledge and Narrative in a Northern Native Community*.

8. I might also add here that Welch mentions yet another kind of distance in the following description: "The country had created a distance as deep as it was empty, and the people accepted and treated each other with distance" (2). However, this distance, which is created by the country, functions as a geographic determinant. Since all people are influenced by it, it forms the background against which the two other more active and individual senses of distance are foregrounded.

9. Tatum continues his discussion using this and other elements of the text to show how the novel separates the signifier from the signified, thus creating a paradox of desire on the personal level for the narrator and one on a more ideological level for the reader. He uses this paradox of desire to reveal how the novel questions the possibility of truth. He sees the novel as a critique of the commodification of gender relations and capitalist ideology. He believes "this narrative's unconscious or immanent project is to disclose the connection between commodities and colonial adventure in an age of empire." (90) While Tatum's analysis serves as a necessary counterweight to more anthropologically oriented criticism, his protean effort both to deny meaning in the text and to promote its radical postmodern message places more weight on dissonances than on the unities. In his

reading, Welch comes off as an Indian protégé of both Jacques Lacan and Terry Eagleton. I doubt that Welch would wish to play such a role.

10. Welch commented on the magpie: "I gave him some human qualities in a sense. I was thinking of him as something more than a bird, you know? Uh-huh, but nothing heavy." (qtd. in Bevis 181)

11. See George Bird Grinnell and Percy Bullchild on Blackfeet views of Napi. It is also interesting to note that some Sioux origin stories present the first man as rising out of the mud. See, for instance, Luther Standing Bear's "Sioux Genesis" quoted in Turner (125).

Chapter 5

1. See Ruoff, "Ritual and Renewal," and Nelson, "Place and Vision."

2. Velie, seeing the dialogism and mediation in the text, attempts to explain them psychologically. He perceives a conflict between a contemporary acculturated mixed-blood Silko and the Indian values of her novel that imply that Natives are best off when they remain in their tradition. To solve the conflict, he refers to Wayne Booth's concept of the implied author, suggesting that Silko can say these things without personally believing in them (Four 113–15). However, perhaps Silko's intent here is just to suggest that mixing contemporary and traditional values will create evolving Native world views that will prove more humane and ecologically sound.

Lincoln suggests that there is a determining level of the text that goes beyond anthropological antecedents: "The narrator *is* the story, positioning, interweaving, toning, speaking for the characters . . . listening to them speak, following their struggles to pattern their lives, according to the old, never-ending Indian "balances and harmonies" (Native 238). However, Lincoln does not define qualities of an individual narrator, nor does he explore the perspective on the text such a narrator would need to take.

3. Appreciating the dialogic nature of Silko's writings can prove useful for many critics. For example, Krupat has applied an appreciation of dialogism and polyvocality in his analysis of Silko's *Storyteller* and in his discussion of Native American autobiography (Voice 132–70; "Dialogic" 55–68).

4. Drawing upon Lacan, Gretchen Ronnow argues that the novel chronicles Tayo's quest across the possibilities of language for a lost mother and a sense of Otherness. This interpretation has value for Silko scholarship because it bridges the gap between the psychological individual inside Tayo and the "something larger" outside of him. However, this bridging of the gap is ultimately not the locus of healing prescribed by Betonie.

5. This discourse field is introduced into the text in enough detail to bring the non-Laguna reader into a mediative posture that will evoke a mythic path for validating experience. A complete analysis of how the novel continues the discourse of Laguna narratives in their own field is outside the scope of this chapter. The contours of Silko's Laguna responses have been outlined by Ruoff ("Ritual"), Hoilman, and Swan ("Laguna"). These authors draw on the ethnographical work of Franz Boas, John Gunn, Hamilton Tyler, and Elsie Crews Parsons.

6. See Kim Barnes, "A Leslie Marmon Silko Interview" (98).

7. Mary Slowik discusses extensively the relation between the poetry and prose sections in the novel and their influence on the reader. While her analysis is hindered by her lack of understanding of the structure and function of Native American oral tradition, she does point to some ways the two narrative modes interrelate. She discusses the way the mythic stories displace and focus the prose narrative and thus create an ironic perspective for the reader. Since the novel reveals that "narrative is ontology" (113), "we now read contrapuntally; that is, as the weave of one story crosses the weave of another" (115). Unfortunately, when she decides that the reader reads the sections concerning the cattle and the Witchery pragmatically, she seems to be ignoring the nature of mythic epistemology.

8. The ceremonial analogues to the novel's process have been extensively explored by Carol Mitchell in "*Ceremony* as Ritual," Robert Bell in "Circular Design in *Ceremony*," and Edith Swan in "Healing via the Sunrise Cycle in Silko's *Ceremony*."

9. Many scholars have commented on this shift of vision at the end of the novel. Robert Nelson observes, "Tayo's vision of the pattern of the ceremony takes a quantum leap of perspective, from Pan-Indian to Pan-Human" (310). Nelson does not follow the implications for the reader of this change. Dasenbrock notes, "Silko relies upon Western forms only to finally have her protagonist break free of them and perceive them as Anglo forms: his perceptions are hers and should be ours" (317). Slowik agrees with some points of my analysis when she writes that in the end, "by allowing us to read two distinct narrative modes, sometimes contradictory narrative modes simultaneously, *Ceremony* ultimately educates us, its readers, to accept the marvelous as readily and as easily as Marquez" (106). Silko's perception is that "storytelling always includes the audience and the listeners, and, in fact, a great deal of the story is believed to be inside the listener, and the storyteller's role is to draw the story out of the listeners" ("Language" 57). The shift of vision at the end would then correspond to the reader's increasing realization that the story is inside him or her.

Chapter 6

1. Velie suggests that *Bearheart* may also be indebted to the road novel. He compares the novel to the work of Rabelais ("Trickster" 129). In a similar vein, Owens mentions "the familiar allegorical pilgrimage a la *Canterbury Tales* but also more pointedly the westerning pattern of American 'discovery' and settlement." He further observes that the novel is "among the most traditional novels by Indian authors" (*Other* 229–30). Keady agrees, noting that while it is "a distinctly 'modern' novel . . . at its core, Vizenor's book is more Indian than western, more saturnalian than satirical" (61). Ruoff perhaps sums it up best when she writes, "Vizenor combines the satire and allegory of classical and Western and Western European epics with the traditions of American Indian oral narratives" ("Woodland" 24).

2. While Vizenor might disagree with the Deconstructionists in many

areas, I think he would sympathize with their emphasis on the indeterminacy of meaning.

3. It is in the context of the necessity of contradiction that we should see many of Vizenor's analytical statements containing words like *wavering* and *between*. Existing in between terminal creeds is the epistemological position of traditional tribal cultures and of many artists, but also it is the position to which Vizenor hopes to move his readers.

4. See Nora Barry, "Chance and Ritual: The Gambler in the Texts of Gerald Vizenor."

5. The example Thompson presents in *Tales of the North American Indians* of a Quinault version of the tale is comparable in many respects to the version Vizenor presents (167–69).

6. Velie argues that the qualities of the traditional Chippewa trickster are allocated separately to Proude and Bigfoot with Proude representing positive attributes and Bigfoot negative ones ("Trickster" 133–35).

7. In *Other Destinies*, Owens implies that Rosina has also transformed into Changing Woman at the end of the novel (240). Allen concludes that Bigfoot has experienced some form of transformation into spirit after his physical death (*Sacred* 97).

Chapter 7

1. In the use of the term *conversation*, Bialostosky is closer to Richard Rorty in *Philosophy and the Mirror of Nature* rather than to Kenneth Burke in *The Philosophy of Literary Forms*.

2. See also Owens, "The 'Map of·the Mind.'"

3. The negotiations with the Heye Foundation Museum of the American Indian are described by Roy Meyer in his *The Village Indians of the Upper Missouri* (205–208). One might even speculate that McNickle modeled Adam Pell on George Heye, founder of the Museum of the American Indian.

4. In his conclusion to *Native American Tribalism*, McNickle specifically cited *Notes* as a pan-tribal political source (169).

5. The letter excerpted here is from the D'Arcy McNickle collection at the Newberry Library.

Chapter 8

1. See Lincoln for a discussion of humor built on oral sources. (*Indi'n* 205–53).

2. In *Indi'n Humor*, Lincoln quotes Erdrich as saying that Indian readers appreciate much of the humor of her book that non-Indian readers miss (239).

3. Brown is in particular discussing Native American attitudes toward place, but as he develops his idea he acknowledges multiple spirits as well as the existence of a universal principle. Consequently, he is forced to define this multiple experiencing of levels of reality. He also discusses the idea of the unity of all being and things.

4. Erdrich may have had an interesting exposure to this "double think." In a television interview with Bill Moyers, Erdrich remembers that her "grandfather was the last person in our family who spoke Ojibwa." His mixture of cultures and epistemologies influenced her, because he "really had a sense of what it was like to grow up before so many changes. . . . He was very Catholic . . ." but prayed in Chippewa. "When I'd be with him, I'd question everything. I felt an entirely different way about religion." Erdrich knew that he used "the very old beliefs that he had to make sense of things." When asked if these beliefs still influenced her, she hesitates, acknowledging that they are a part of her but so "subterranean, that probably it comes out mainly in the writing . . . I'm not sure ("Conversation").

5. In her otherwise valuable article, Rainwater does not consider the responses of a Native reader, nor acknowledge that the existence of such an audience might influence not only the text but also the nature of the marginalization required of the reader. For her, the final position of the disempowered reader is one of equating story and reality. However, this is not a "between worlds" position that resists "any interpretative urge which is founded on epistemological or theological certainty" (413). Rather the point that she misses is that it is a more Native epistemological position; it protects the core of culture.

6. Landes discusses the necessity of vision, religious preparation, and continual discussion of spiritual purpose for a successful war party. Landes also notes that some Ojibwa contend that the souls of warriors who had been scalped or beheaded were prone to wander the land between the human world and the ghost village. Other writers have commented that the souls of those who have drowned must also wander forever.

7. For information on water spirits, see both Van Dyke and Vecsey (74).

8. Barnouw also notes the "curious equation between hunting and courting" in Chippewa language and social custom (248).

9. I agree with Rainwater here but not with her view that code of identity is based on natural elements. Claims Rainwater, "Especially in *Love Medicine,* characters are formed through various syntagmatic series of references to natural elements such as air, earth, fire, and water" (421). This seems to me as tantamount to equating Native American concepts of identity with ancient Greek philosophy. Closer to my point is Jeanne Smith's insight that "in *Love Medicine,* characters build identity on transpersonal connections to community, to landscape, and to myth" (13), though Keith Basso, Robin Riddington, and others have also shown that identity connections to landscape are created in the context of community and myth.

10. The name of the trickster varies in much of Chippewa literature. Landes records it as *Nehnehbush.*

Works Cited

◆

Allen, Paula Gunn. "American Indian Fiction, 1968–1983." *A Literary History of the American West*. Fort Worth: Texas Christian University Press, 1987.

————. *The Sacred Hoop: Recovering the Feminine in American Indian Traditions*. Boston: Beacon Press, 1986.

Arendt, Hannah. *Between Past and Future: Six Exercises in Political Thought*. 1954. New York: Meridian, 1963.

Bakhtin, Mikhail. *The Dialogic Imagination: Four Essays by M. M. Bakhtin*. Ed. Michael Holquist. Austin and London: University of Texas Press, 1981.

Ballard, Charles. "The Theme of the Helping Hand in *Winter in the Blood*." *MELUS* 17.1 (1991–92): 63–75.

Barnes, Kim. "A Leslie Marmon Silko Interview with Kim Barnes." *Journal of Ethnic Studies* 13.4 (1986): 83–105.

Barnouw, Victor. *Wisconsin Chippewa Myths & Tales and Their Relation to Chippewa Life*. Madison: University of Wisconsin Press, 1977.

Barry, Nora. "Chance and Ritual: The Gambler in the Texts of Gerald Vizenor." *SAIL: Studies in American Indian Literatures* 5.3 (1993): 13–22.

Basso, Keith. *Western Apache Language and Culture: Essays in Linguistic Anthropology*. Tucson: University of Arizona Press, 1990.

Bataille, Gretchen. "Transformation of Tradition: Autobiographical Works by American Indian Women." *Studies in American Indian Literature: Critical Essays and Course Designs*. Ed. Paula Allen. New York: Modern Language Association, 1983. 85–99.

Bell, Robert C. "Circular Design in *Ceremony*." *American Indian Quarterly* 5 (1979): 47–62.

Bevis, Bill. "Dialogue with James Welch." *Northwest Review* 20.2–3 (1982): 163–85.

Bevis, William. "Native American Novels: Homing In." *Recovering the Word: Essays on Native American Literature.* Eds. Brian Swann and Arnold Krupat. Berkeley: University of California Press, 1987. 580–621.

Bialostosky, Don H. "Dialogics as an Art of Discourse in Literary Criticism." *Publications of the Modern Language Association* 101 (1986): 788–97.

Black Elk. *Black Elk Speaks.* Ed. John Neihardt. 1932. New York: Washington Square, 1972.

Booth, Wayne. *Rhetoric of Fiction.* Chicago: University of Chicago Press, 1961.

Brown, Joseph Epes. "The Roots of Renewal." *Seeing with a Native Eye: Essays on Native American Relgiion.* Ed. Walter H. Capps. New York: Harper & Row, 1976.

Bruchac, Joseph. *Survival This Way: Interviews with American Indian Poets.* Tucson: University of Arizona Press, 1987.

Bullchild, Percy. *The Sun Came Down.* San Francisco: Harper & Row, 1985.

Burke, Kenneth. *The Philosophy of Literary Forms: Studies in Symbolic Action.* Rev. Ed. New York: Vintage Press, 1957.

Clifford, James. *The Predicament of Culture: Twentieth-Century Ethnography, Literature, and Art.* Cambridge: Harvard University Press, 1988.

Coltelli, Laura, ed. *Winged Words: American Indian Writers Speak.* Lincoln: University of Nebraska Press, 1990.

"A Conversation with Louise Erdrich and Michael Dorris." *A World of Ideas with Bill Moyers* PBS. WNET, New York. 1990.

Cove, John. *Shattered Images: Dialogues and Meditations on Tsimshian Narratives.* Ottawa: Carleton University Press, 1987.

Craig, David M. "Beyond Assimilation: James Welch and the Indian Dilemma." *North Dakota Quarterly* 53 (1985): 183–90.

Dasenbrock, Reed Way. "Forms of Biculturalism in Southwestern Literature: The Work of Rudolfo Anaya and Leslie Marmon Silko." *Genre* 21 (1988): 307–20.

Deloria, Vine, Jr. *Custer Died for Your Sins: An Indian Manifesto.* New York: Avon, 1969.

Dunsmore, Roger. "Reflections on *Wind From an Enemy Sky* and 'killing the water.'" *SAIL: Studies in American Indian Literatures* 11.1 (1987): 38–56.

Erdrich, Louise. *Love Medicine.* 1984. New York: Bantam, 1987.

———. "Where I Ought to Be: A Writer's Sense of Place," *New York Times* 28 July 1985, sec. 7: 1+.

Eliade, Mircea. *Myth and Reality.* Trans. Willard Trask. New York: Harper & Row, 1963.

———. *The Myth of the Eternal Return.* Trans. Willard Trask. New York: Pantheon Books, 1954.

———. *The Sacred and the Profane: The Nature of Religion.* Trans. Willard Trask. 1959. New York: Harper & Row, 1973.

Evers, Lawrence. "Words and Place: A Reading of *House Made of Dawn.*" *Critical Essays on Native American Literature.* Ed. Andrew Wiget. Boston: G. K. Hall, 1985. 211–229.

Fischer, Michael M. J. "Ethnicity and the Post-Modern Arts of Memory." *Writing Culture: The Poetics and Politics of Ethnography.* Eds. James

Clifford and George E. Marcus. Berkeley: University of California Press, 1986. 194–233.

Forbes, Jack D. "Determining Who Is an Indian." *Amerika Studien* 24 (1983): 404–16.

Geertz, Clifford. "From the Native's Point of View: On the Nature of Anthropological Understanding." *Culture Theory: Essays on Mind, Self and Emotion.* Eds. Richard Shweder and Robert LeVine. Cambridge: Cambridge University Press, 1984. 123–36.

Genette, Gerard. *Narrative Discourse Revisited.* Trans. Jane E. Lewin. 1983. Ithaca: Cornell University Press, 1988.

Gish, Robert. "Mystery and Mock Intrigue in James Welch's *Winter in the Blood.*" *James Welch.* Ed. Ron McFarland. Confluence American Authors Series 1. Lewiston: Confluence Press, 1986. 45–57.

Grinnell, George Bird. *Blackfoot Lodge Tales.* 1892. Lincoln: University of Nebraska Press, 1962.

Hallowell, A. Irving. "Ojibwa Ontology, Behavior, and World View." *Culture in History: Essays in Honor of Paul Radin.* Ed. Stanley Diamond. New York: Columbia University Press, 1960. 13–52.

Hassan, Ihab. *Radical Innocence: Studies in the Contemporary Novel.* Princeton: Princeton University Press, 1961.

Hirsch, Bernard. "Self-Hatred and Spiritual Corruption in *House Made of Dawn.*" *Western American Literature* 17.4 (1983): 307–24.

Hobson, Geary. Introduction. *The Remembered Earth: An Anthology of Contemporary Native American Literature.* Ed. Geary Hobson. 1979. Albuquerque: University of New Mexico Press, 1981.

Hogan, Linda. "Who Puts Together." *Studies in American Indian Literature: Critical Essays and Course Designs.* Ed. Paula Allen. New York: Modern Language Association, 1983. 169–77.

Hoilman, Dennis. "A World Made of Stories: An Interpretation of Leslie Silko's *Ceremony.*" *South Dakota Review* 17 (1979–80): 54–66.

Horton, Andrew. "The Bitter Humor of *Winter in the Blood.*" *American Indian Quarterly* 4 (1978): 131–39.

Iser, Wolfgang. *The Act of Reading.* Baltimore: Johns Hopkins University, 1978.

Jacobs, Melville. *The Content and Style of an Oral Literature: Clackmas Chinook Myths and Tales.* Chicago: University of Chicago Press, 1959.

Jahner, Elaine. "An Act of Attention: Event Structure in *Ceremony.*" *American Indian Quarterly* 5.1 (1979): 37–46.

———. "A Critical Approach to American Indian Literatures." *Studies in American Indian Literature: Critical Essays and Course Designs.* Ed. Paula Allen. New York: Modern Language Association, 1983. 211–24.

———. "Cultural Shrines Revisited." *American Indian Quarterly* 9.1 (1986): 23–30.

———. "Quick Paces And A Space of Mind." *Denver Quarterly* 14.4 (1980): 34–47.

James, Henry. "The Art of Fiction." *The Future of the Novel: Essays on the Art of Fiction.* Ed. Leon Edel. New York: Vintage, 1956.

Keady, Maureen. "Walking Backwards into the Fourth World: Survival of the Fittest in *Bearheart*." *American Indian Quarterly* 9.1 (1986): 61–65.

Kerr, Baine. "The Novel as Sacred Text: N. Scott Momaday's Myth-Making Ethic." *Southwest Review* 63.2 (Spring 1978): 172–79.

Kristeva, Julia. *Language—the Unknown: an Initiation into Linguistics.* New York: Columbia University Press, 1989.

Krupat, Arnold. "The Dialogic of Silko's *Storyteller*." *Narrative Chance: Postmodern Discourse on Native American Indian Literatures.* Ed. Gerald Vizenor. Albuquerque: University of New Mexico Press, 1989.

———. *Ethnocriticism: Ethnography, History, Literature.* Berkeley: University of California Press, 1992.

———. *The Voice in the Margin: Native American Literature and the Canon.* Berkeley: University of California Press, 1989.

Kunz, Don. "Lost in the Distance of Winter: James Welch's *Winter in the Blood*." *Critique* 20.1 (1978): 93–99.

Landes, Ruth. *Ojibway Religion and the Midewiwin.* Madison: University of Wisconsin Press, 1968.

———. *Ojibway Sociology.* 1937. New York: AMS Press, 1969.

Larson, Charles. *American Indian Fiction.* Albuquerque: University of New Mexico Press, 1978.

Larson, Sidner. "Native American Aesthetics: An Attitude of Relationship." *MELUS* 17.3 (1991–92): 53–68.

Lincoln, Kenneth. "Bad Jokes, Short Words, Stunted Psyches and Debatable Humor in *Winter in the Blood*." *Native American Literatures.* Ed. Laura Coltelli. Pisa, Italy: University of Pisa, 1989.

———. "Common Walls: The Poetry of Simon Ortiz." *Coyote Was Here: Essays on Contemporary Native American Literary and Political Mobilization.* Ed. Bo Scholer. Aarhus, Denmark: Seklos, 1984.

———. *Indi'n Humor: Bicultural Play in Native America.* New York: Oxford University Press, 1993.

———. *Native American Renaissance.* Berkeley: University of California Press, 1983.

Lyotard, Jean-François. *The Post-Modern Condition: A Report on Knowledge.* Minneapolis: University of Minnesota, 1984.

Marcus, George E. "Contemporary Problems of Ethnography in the Modern World System." *Writing Culture: The Poetics and Politics of Ethnography.* Eds. James Clifford and George E. Marcus. Berkeley: University of California Press, 1986.

Martin, Calvin. *American Indian and the Problem of History* New York: Oxford University Press, 1987.

Martin, Wallace. *Recent Theories of Narrative.* Ithaca: Cornell University Press, 1986.

McNickle, D'Arcy. *The Indian Tribes of the United States: Ethnic and Cultural Survival.* 1962. Rpt. as *Native American Tribalism: Indian Renewals and Survivals.* New York: Oxford University Press, 1973.

———. *Indians and Other Americans: A Study of Indian Affairs.* 1959. New York: Harper, 1970.

———. Letter to Dr. Sol Tax 29 March 1972. D'Arcy McNickle Papers. Newberry Library, Chicago.

———. *The Surrounded*. 1936. Albuquerque: University of New Mexico Press, 1978.

———. *Wind From an Enemy Sky*. San Francisco: Harper & Row, 1978.

Meyer, Roy. *The Village Indians of the Upper Missouri: The Mandans, Hidatsas, and Arikaras*. Lincoln: University of Nebraska Press, 1977.

Mitchell, Carol. "Ceremony as Ritual." *American Indian Quarterly* 5 (1979): 27–35.

Momaday, N. Scott. *Ancestral Voices: Conversations with N. Scott Momaday*. Ed. Charles Woodard. Lincoln: University of Nebraska Press, 1989.

———. *House Made of Dawn*. New York: Harper, 1968.

———. "Man Made of Words." *Literatures of the American Indians: Views and Interpretations*. Ed. Abraham Chapman. Meridian: New York, 1975. 96–110.

———. "The Morality of Indian Hating." *Ramparts* 3 (1964): 30–34.

———. "Native American Attitudes to the Environment." *Seeing with a Native Eye: Essays on Native American Religion*. Ed. Walter Capps. New York: Harper & Row, 1976. 79–85.

Nelson, Richard K. *Make Prayers to the Raven: A Koyukon View of the Northern Forest*. Chicago: University of Chicago Press, 1983.

Nelson, Robert. "Place and Vision: The Function of Landscape in *Ceremony*." *Journal of the Southwest* 30.3 (1988): 281–316.

———. "Snake and Eagle: Abel's Disease and the Landscape of *House Made of Dawn*." *SAIL: Studies in American Indian Literatures* 1.2 (1989): 1–20.

Oleson, Carole. "The Remembered Earth: Momaday's *House Made of Dawn*." *South Dakota Review*, 11.1 (1973): 59–78.

Ortiz, Alfonso. "American Indian Philosophy." *Indian Voices: the First Convocation of American Indian Scholars*. San Francisco: Indian Historian Press, 1970.

Ortiz, Simon. "That's the Place Indians Talk About." *The Wicazo Sa Review* 1.1 (1985): 45–49.

———. "Toward a National Indian Literature: Cultural Authenticity in Nationalism." *MELUS* 8.2 (1981): 7–12.

Owens, Louis. Afterword. *Bearheart: The Heirship Chronicles*. By Gerald Vizenor. Minneapolis: University of Minnesota Press, 1990. 247–54.

———. "The 'Map of the Mind': D'Arcy McNickle and the American Indian Novel." *Western American Literature* 19 (1984): 275–83.

———. *Other Destinies: Understanding the American Indian Novel*. Norman: University of Oklahoma Press, 1992.

Parsons, Elsie Crews. *The Pueblo of Jemez*. New Haven: Yale University Press, 1925.

Pratt, Mary Louise. "Arts of the Contact Zone." *Profession* (1991): 33–40.

Purdy, John. *Word Ways: The Novels of D'Arcy McNickle*. Tucson: University of Arizona Press, 1990.

Rainwater, Catherine. "Reading between Worlds: Narrativity in the Fiction of Louise Erdrich." *American Literature* 62.3 (1990): 405–22.

Ridington, Robin. "Models of the Universe: The Poetic Paradigm of Benjamin Lee Whorf." *Anthropology and Humanism Quarterly* 12 (1987): 16–24.

———. *Trail to Heaven: Knowledge and Narrative in a Northern Native Community.* Iowa City: University of Iowa Press, 1988.

Rigal-Cellard, Bernadette. "A Reading of the Prologue of *House Made of Dawn* by N. Scott Momaday." *Native American Literatures. Forum* 2–3 (1990–91): 39–56.

Ronnow, Gretchen. "Tayo, Death, and Desire: A Lacanian Reading of *Ceremony.*" *Narrative Chance: Postmodern Discourse on Native American Indian Literatures.* Ed. Gerald Vizenor. Albuquerque: University of New Mexico Press, 1989.

Rorty, Richard. *Philosophy and the Mirror of Nature.* Princeton: Princeton University Press, 1979.

Rosen, Kenneth. "American Indian Literature: Current Condition and Suggested Research." *American Indian Culture and Research Journal* 3.2 (1979): 57–66.

Ruoff, A. LaVonne. "Alienation and the Female Principle in *Winter in the Blood.*" *American Indian Quarterly* 4.2 (1978): 107–122.

———. "Ritual and Renewal: Keres Traditions in the Short Fiction of Leslie Silko." *Multi-Ethnic Literatures of the United States* 5 (1978): 2–17.

———. "Woodland Word Warrior: An Introduction to the Works of Gerald Vizenor." *Multi-Ethnic Literatures of the United States* 13. 1–2 (1986): 13–43.

Ruppert, James. "Mediation and Multiple Narrative in Contemporary Native American Fiction." *Texas Studies in Literature and Language* 26 (1986): 209–25.

Sanders, Scott. "Review of *Love Medicine.*" *Studies in American Indian Literature* 9.1 (1985): 6–10.

Sands, Kay. "Alienation and Broken Narrative in *Winter in the Blood.*" *American Indian Quarterly* 4.2 (1978): 97–105.

———. "American Indian Autobiography." *Studies in American Indian Literature: Critical Essays and Course Designs.* Ed. Paula Allen. New York: Modern Language Association, 1983. 55–65.

———. "Review of *Love Medicine.*" *SAIL: Studies in American Indian Literatures* 9.1 (1985): 12–24.

Scarberry-Garcia, Susan. *Landmarks of Healing: A Study of House Made of Dawn.* Albuquerque: University of New Mexico Press, 1990.

Schneider, Jack. "The New Indian: Alienation and the Rise of the Indian Novel." *South Dakota Review* 17 (1979–80): 67–76.

Schubnell, Matthias. *N. Scott Momaday.* Norman: University of Oklahoma Press, 1985.

Sheldon, Mary F. "Reaching for a Universal Audience: The Artistry of Leslie Marmon Silko and James Welch." *Entering the 90s: The North American Experience.* Ed. Thomas Schirer. Sault Ste. Marie: Lake Superior State University, 1989.

Silberman, Robert. "Opening the Text: *Love Medicine* and the Return of the Native American Woman." *Narrative Chance: Postmodern Discourse on Native American Indian Literatures.* Ed. Gerald Vizenor. Albuquerque:

University of New Mexico, 1989.

Silko, Leslie. *Ceremony.* New York: Signet, 1977.

———. "A Conversation with Leslie Marmon Silko." Larry Evers and Denny Carr, Eds. *Suntracks* 3 (1976): 28–33.

———. "Language and Literature from a Pueblo Indian Perspective." *English Literature: Opening Up the Canon.* Eds. Leslie Fiedler and Houston Baker. Baltimore: Johns Hopkins University Press, 1981. 54–72.

———. "Stories and Their Tellers: A Conversation with Leslie Marmon Silko." *The Third Woman: Minority Women Writers of the United States.* Ed. Dexter Fisher. New York: Houghton Mifflin, 1980. 18–23.

Seyersted, Per. *Leslie Marmon Silko.* Western Writers Series. Boise: Boise State University Press, 1980.

Slowik, Mary. "Henry James, Meet Spider Woman: A Study of Narrative Form in Leslie Silko's *Ceremony.*" *North Dakota Quarterly* 57.2 (1989): 104–20.

Smith, Jeanne. "Transpersonal Selfhood: The Boundaries of Identity in Louise Erdrich's *Love Medicine.*" *SAIL: Studies in American Indian Literatures* 3.4 (1991): 13–26.

Stanzel, Franz. *A Theory of Narrative.* Trans. Charlotte Goedsche. Cambridge: Cambridge University Press, 1984.

Strelke, Barbara. "N. Scott Momaday: Racial Memory and Individual Imagination." *Literatures of the American Indians: Views and Interpretations.* Ed. Abraham Chapman. New York: Meridian, 1975. 348–357.

Swan, Edith. "Healing via the Sunwise Cycle." *American Indian Quarterly* 12.3 (1988): 229–49.

———. "Laguna Symbolic Geography and Silko's *Ceremony.*" *American Indian Quarterly* 12.4 (1988): 313–28.

Tatum, Stephen. " 'Distance,' Desire, and the Ideological Matrix of *Winter in the Blood.*" *Arizona Quarterly* 46.2 (1990): 73–100.

Tedlock, Dennis. *The Spoken Word and the Work of Interpretation.* Philadelphia: University of Pennsylvania Press, 1983.

Thackeray, William. " 'Crying for Pity' in *Winter in the Blood.*" *MELUS* 7.1 (1980): 61–78.

Thompson, Stith. *The Folktale.* New York: The Dryden Press, 1951.

———. *Tales of the North American Indian.* 1929. Bloomington: Indiana University Press, 1966.

Toelken, Barre. "Seeing with a Native Eye: How Many Sheep Will It Hold." *Seeing with a Native Eye: Essays on Native American Religion.* Ed. Walter Capps. New York: Harper & Row, 1976.

Todorov, Tzvetan. *Mikhail Bakhtin: The Dialogical Principle.* Trans. Wlad Godzich. Minneapolis: University of Minnesota Press, 1984.

———. *The Poetics of Prose.* Trans. Richard Howard. Ithaca: Cornell University Press, 1977.

Trimble, Martha. *N. Scott Momaday.* Western Writers Series 9. Boise: Boise State College, 1973.

Trimmer, Joseph. "Native Americans and the American Mix: N. Scott Momaday's *House Made Of Dawn.*" *Indiana Social Studies Quarterly* 28 (1975): 75–91.

Turner, Frederick W., III, ed. *The Portable North American Indian Reader*. New York: Viking, 1974.

Tyler, Stephen. "Postmodern Anthropology." *Discourse and the Social Life of Meaning*. Eds. Phyllis Pease Chock and June Wyman. Washington: Smithsonian Institution Press, 1986. 23–49.

Van Dyke, Annette. "Questions of the Spirit: Bloodlines in Louise Erdrich's Chippewa Landscape." *SAIL: Studies in American Indian Literatures* 4.1 (1992): 15–27.

Vangen, Kate. "Making Faces: Defiance and Humor in Campbell's *Halfbreed* and Welch's *Winter in the Blood*." *The Native in Literature*. Eds. Thomas King, et al. Oakville, Ontario: ECW Press, 1987. 188–205.

Vecsey, Christopher. *Traditional Ojibwa Religion and Its Historical Changes*. Philadelphia: The American Philosophical Society, 1983.

Velie, Alan. *Four American Indian Literary Masters: N. Scott Momaday, James Welch, Leslie Marmon Silko and Gerald Vizenor*. Norman: University of Oklahoma Press, 1982.

———. "The Trickster Novel." *Narrative Chance: Postmodern Discourse on Native American Indian Literatures*. Ed. Gerald Vizenor. Albuquerque: University of New Mexico Press, 1989. 121–39.

Vizenor, Gerald. *Crossbloods: Bone Courts, Bingo, and Other Reports*. Minneapolis: University of Minnesota Press, 1990.

———. *Darkness in St. Louis Bearheart*. 1978. Rpt. as *Bearheart: The Heirship Chronicles*. Minneapolis: University of Minnesota Press, 1990.

———. *Earthdivers: Tribal Narratives on Mixed Descent*. Minneapolis: University of Minnesota Press, 1981.

———. "Gerald Vizenor." *This Song Remembers: Self-Portraits of Native Americans in the Arts*. Ed. Jane Katz. Boston: Houghton Mifflin, 1980.

———. "GERALD VIZENOR: The Trickster Heir of Columbus, AN INTERVIEW." *Native American Literatures*. Ed. Laura Coltelli. *Forum* (Pisa) 2–3 (1990–91): 101–116.

———. *The People Named the Chippewa: Narrative Histories*. Minneapolis: University of Minnesota Press, 1984.

———. "A Postmodern Introduction." *Narrative Chance: Postmodern Discourse on Native American Indian Literatures*. Ed. Gerald Vizenor. Albuquerque: University of New Mexico Press, 1989. 3–16.

———. "Trickster Discourse: Comic Holotropes and Language Games." *Narrative Chance: Postmodern Discourse on Native American Literatures*. Albuquerque: University of New Mexico Press, 1989. 187–211.

———. *The Trickster of Liberty: Tribal Heirs to a Wild Baronage*. Minneapolis: University of Minnesota, 1988.

Wagner, Roy. *The Invention of Culture*. Chicago and London: University of Chicago Press, 1975.

Waniek, Marilyn. "The Power of Language in N. Scott Momaday's *House Made of Dawn*." *Minority Voices* 4.1 (1980): 23–28.

Welch, James. "A Conversation with James Welch." *South Dakota Review* 28.1 (1990): 103–10.

———. *Winter in the Blood*. 1974. New York: Penguin, 1988.

White, Hayden. *Tropics of Discourse: Essays in Cultural Criticism.* Baltimore and London: Johns Hopkins University Press, 1978.

Whorf, Benjamin Lee. "An American Indian Model of the Universe." *Teachings from the American Earth: Indian Religion and Philosophy.* Eds. Dennis and Barbara Tedlock. New York: Liveright, 1975. 121–29.

Wiget, Andrew. Foreword. *Landmarks of Healing: A Study of House Made of Dawn.* By Susan Scarberry-Garcia. Albuquerque: University of New Mexico Press, 1990.

———. "Identity, Voice, and Authority: Artist-Audience Relations in Native American Literature." *World Literature Today* 66.2 (1992): 258–63.

———. *Native American Literature.* Boston: Twayne, 1985.

Index